DUAL

NOTHING IS WHAT IT SEEMS

Marshall Ericho

Papua New Guinea

Paperback ISBN: 978-1-7638456-4-0

First Published in 2025 by
First Nations Writers Festival International Limited
T/as First Nations Publishers

A Registered Charity (ABN 79 655 932 979)

2/53 Junction St, Nowra NSW 2540, Australia
Phone: +61 491 851 353

Email: firstnationswritersfestival@gmail.com
Web: www.firstnationswritersfestival.org
FB: www.facebook.com/firstnationswritersfestival.com

Cover Design: Busybird Publishing
Typeset: Busybird Publishing
Cover Photo: Marshall Ericho
Line Edited: Anna Borzi AM 2025

Printed and bound in Australia by IngramSpark. Thus book is a woork of fiction.
Names, characters, places and incidents are products of the author's imagination of or
are used fictitiously. This includes the fictional Kundiawa Bank. Any resemblance to actual
events or locales of persons, living or dead, is entirely coincidental.
References to historical recounts, culture, rivers, mountains,
and places are entirely factual (as are their exact location).
Kundiawa Town is also factual.

Papua New Guinea

A catalogue record fpor this book is available from the National Library of Australia

PROLOGUE

Maria launched herself at an intersection, cartwheeling across the limestone dirt road, from the V8 that was going 50 miles per hour. She blacked out.

Jim Rento made a hard brake, "what the fu-"

The opened door slammed shut!

"Go!" Oscar shouted. Jim stepped on the accelerator again. He didn't stop to see if Maria was alright, the idea was to get the door shut all by itself by coming to an abrupt halt when the vehicle was in motion, because he sure as hell wasn't going to lean over and waste time closing the door.

They could hear the police sirens nearing.

"Brave woman!" Jim Rento said. "What was she thinking?!"

"Casualty of war," Oscar said, coldly. "When it rains, everyone gets wet."

Al Simon stood-up on his right knee on the car seat, and turned around to see where Maria had landed through the shattered back windscreen. As he did so he noticed something else and let out a distraught groan, "No no no!"

Oscar immediately stood on his knees as well and turned. When Oscar saw what Al Simon was looking at, he knew their problems had just gotten worse.

"What is it?" Jim Rento asked. Oscar and Al Simon exchanged sceptic looks. The V8 had already rounded the bend at Dogor. Oscar knew it was the perfect spot for an ambush if the police in Mirane intended to do one.

"What the hell is it?!" Jim Rento shouted with rage. Oscar was hesitant, "Mikes, Mikes is gone -" Before Oscar could complete, he spotted armed men in blue uniforms moving inconspicuously amongst the roadside reeds all around the bend. The vehicle slowed down.

Jim Rento somehow no longer had the will to carry on, he lowered his head and started sobbing.

Chapter 1

Dua and his grandmother had faced the drought together on a secluded barren mountaintop; in their old, dried up, Kunai Grass home, the only hamlet in sight for miles around.

That afternoon, Dua stood near the Southern Cliffside looking down the gorge. He stood shirtless in rugged short jeans. His body glimmers revealing well defined muscles. A lifetime of putting up with his harsh mountainous environment earned him a naturally ripped body.

All around as far as the eyes could see colossal mountains rise and fall. The term *mountainous region* couldn't better sum up the description of Chimbu Province. On the west, the blood red afternoon sun retired behind the Mountains of Gumuni. A drowsy silence lay over the whole land. On eye level, Kundiawa Town began to lightened up. Dua often imagined that if there was a foot bridge from where he stood to Kundiawa Town, he could be in Town in less than five minutes instead of walking down to Wara Simbu, and the agonising climb all the way back up.

Dua turned to face his grandmother, "Grandma what if it doesn't rain for another month?"

"If it is the will of God then so be it," said Grandma.

"Maybe God has forgotten us".

"Stop this, Dua! If you want to leave this place and go, I am not stopping you, I can fend for myself!" Grandma said, loudly.

"You won't survive a day out here on your own. I am the only person standing between you and death," Dua retorts, angrily. "I could venture out and live my life carefree like most young men my age, but I choose to be trapped here just because of you."

There was a long, pained silence.

"I am sorry Dua, I know if it wasn't for you I would have already perished. I owe you this much," Grandma said, quietly.

"No Grandma, you don't owe me anything. I owe you everything. I am sorry, I spoke out of context, forgive me."

"That's right, now you are coming to your senses. I raised you up from a defenseless infant to a boy, and now, just look at the man you have become, you are exactly what I wanted, and that is all that should matter to you," said Grandma. Grandma moved closer to Dua this time, and said in a whisper, as if telling a secret.

"Look, I understand why you have been tense lately," she said. "Just like this ground desperately needs water, you also desperately need a female companion. You suffer from lack of sex."

"Please, enough. Enough with the wife subject, I don't need one." Dua cuts in, irritated.

Grandma looked up, disappointed. "You said that a year ago and I'm still waiting here."

"Keep waiting," Dua chortled and walked away towards the house trying to avoid the discussion. Times have changed. Grandma was still trapped in her own time-zone where finding a partner meant waltzing to another village and bride without establishing any form of relationship or na or engagement as they call it. Randomly select intimacy, the ambuya.

Dua would often remark that the whole idea was absurd, but that afternoon he was too tired to start another debate with Grandma. He looked exhausted as he stood in front of the hamlet. He called over to Grandma to bring the house key which she always wears around her neck with a lace.

It had been yet another hectic day at the riverside garden; Dua was already hungry and tired. Grandma sluggishly got on her feet and walked over with a bilum of kapiak leaves and fern which they had collected beside Waghi River basin. Grandma was still complaining about Dua's need for a wife as she came over, but Dua wasn't paying attention.

Dua's mind drifted off, he felt as if something was rank in the void; missing. Dua stared blindly.

"What's eating you? Have you forgotten something?" Grandma enquired. Dua turned to face his grandmother, startled. Grandma observed curiously, "you seem distant all of a sudden."

"I just have this feeling something is missing," Dua said, looking around, "it's probably nothing, I'm hungry, my mind's a bit slow to remember."

"I'll tell you what's missing?"

"What?"

"A wife! That's what's missing around here."

"Just open the door please."

Grandma continued sulking as she carefully removed the lace around her neck which she used to secure the house key. She inserted the key inside the lock's keyhole with shaky hands; struggling to see the key hole. It was already getting dark. She removed the lock after successfully unlocking it, slams the rusty old winches back, and pushed open the door. The door cried like a groaning old man; reaching out to greet them.

Dua ushered his grandmother through and followed right after. Home sweet home. Familiar smoky odour, charging inside whilst she was still moving inside.

The hamlet was lifeless and dark as a cave. But they both knew exactly where to stand and move around. The central fireplace came alive as Grandma fiddled the ashes with a stick to see the still burning orange charcoals.

She continuously blew on the burning exposed charcoal till it produced flame, then she quickly but gently placed bits and pieces of wood – slowly increasing the size of the wood as the flame matures. In less than two minutes the whole interior of the hamlet was exposed.

The hamlet's interior was oval shaped. Dried corn and peanut seeds hung from the roof's crossbar up top that supported the thatched roof. One corner had been separated with walls woven from special cane stalks to form a small room. Dua slept in that room. Grandma has the whole fireplace area to herself.

Right next to the door stood the only furniture inside their home – a table which Dua had constructed out of bamboo. The table had two compartments, the lower one was used to place pots, and the upper one used for plates and cups. The cane woven wall supporting the table had forks, spoons and knives holstered on to it.

An irrelevant picture of a happy looking white family beside the beach stripped out from an old Women's Weekly Magazine was attached to the wall beside the table. Grandma would often come to that corner and describe how happy they all looked, especially the children; she would describe the children's face and laugh at her own remarks while Dua watched.

Dua sat beside the fireplace relishing the heat while Grandma moved inside the hut gracefully like a cat to prepare dinner. Greater extremes in temperatures had been one of the effects of the drought, with very cold nights and frosts which occurred as night time temperatures fell below the hot days and freezing in the high altitude parts of the province.

Grandma brought to light the bounty from whatever they had managed to forage beside Waghi River basin that day. From inside tightly enclosed banana leaves she gently unwrapped the parcel to reveal mushrooms and beans. Grandma carefully inspected the mushrooms again one by one to make sure none of them were lethal.

Dua watched closely the inspection, knowing how important it is to be one hundred per cent certain that it was the right mushroom before consuming it. Mushrooms with hallucinogenic properties the 'Psilocybe' species had been responsible for the 'Mushroom madness' all along the banks of Waghi River.

Satisfied that all the mushrooms were edible Grandma asked Dua to bring a bowl of water to wash the dirt off the mushrooms. Dua indolently got on his feet to attend to the task at hand.

But, before Dua took the first step Grandma let out a horrified shriek! Dua's heart leapt, in dismay and a frightful look swept across his face. "What is it!".

"Dua!" Grandma cried, "I think I know what's been eating you!"

"What is it?"

"We left Mona still tied down at the garden! We forgot to bring Mona!"

Oh my God! Dua thought. Without uttering another word Dua instantaneously dashed out of the door as if the hamlet's roof was on fire.

Chapter 2

Dua ran down the mountain in the same direction he had come up earlier. The dark gradually ate away whatever morsel of light the retiring sun could spare. Going down was much easier and less effort, but if he lost sight of the path or control he could easily run over the edge and fall to his death.

In less than ten minutes Dua arrived at the garden beside the Waghi River on the base of the mountain. Dua wasn't wasting any time; he went right to the spot where Mona was tied up. Mona was nowhere in sight.

Dua panicked but assured himself that Mona was sure to be behind the bushes; so Dua started grunting. He kept grunting as he knelt forward trying to locate the leash. He combed the lower shrubs with both hands until he felt a tight rope inside the grass.

Dua was relieved for the moment but still Mona was nowhere to be seen. Dua followed the line, grunting and pulling, certain that it will lead directly to Mona's right foot.

Suddenly, Dua's grunting is acknowledged by another grunt nearby, underneath a cluster of reeds that slept sideways, creating a hollow shelter. Dua sighed with relief as he stood there yanking the leash and grunting much quicker this time. His grunting is echoed by the pig from where it hid.

The pig slowly came out, grunting and swinging its tail from side to side. Dua was pleased to see Mona, and he was certain the animal felt the same way. Dua often found it ironic that his grandmother would name the pig – why would you name a pig and get emotionally attached to it when eventually you will slaughter it mercilessly when the need arises?

Dua yanked the pig by the leash towards him and pets its head to assure the animal that he had come back to take her home. The animal complied. Dua led as Mona followed closely behind to the stem where the other end of the rope's tied.

Dua struggled to untie the rope now. He was already exhausted. He stood up to recuperate.

The crescent moon hung low over the mountains and reflected on the glassy river's surface. Waghi River, the main artery of the lower Highlands Region, once murky, swift and impossible to cross had now shrunk and flowed gracefully. Grandma had crossed the river earlier that day and stressed how a year ago she would have been submerged and dragged underneath by the swirls until her lifeless body surfaced further downstream.

Now, standing there Dua shook his head and looked away from the river. The trees all around him came alive with awkward humanlike figures – dancing in the wind. At that moment Dua felt like he was being watched. Fear began to creep in; the fear of being alone in the dark.

Dua gripped the leash and motioned Mona with grunts, we need to get out of here. He yanked Mona's leash and knelt down to untie the constricted end on the stump, as he knelt the corner of his right eye caught a glimpse of a rather illusive figure beside the river.

Dua turned immediately to establish his regard. Dua vaguely worked out what it was; it seemed to appear as a tree stump, but Dua did not remember seeing a tree stump there before. This appeared out of nowhere, he thought.

Dua struggled to summon his courage, this is just a tree stump, it's not even mov – before Dua could make any more assumptions the figure beside the river started shifting its shape; it was slowly moving, moving, and when it finally stopped moving, a ghastly figure of a man now stood beside the river. A ghost!

Dua gasped. Fear consumed him.

Chapter 3

Mona ran back into the bush yanking Dua's right arm back. The sheer strength of the animal flung Dua backwards and he fell hard on the ground. The leash was still wrapped around Dua's right arm, straining his wrist as the animal struggled to escape.

Dua rolled over on his belly and got to his feet while grabbing the leash with both hands dragging Mona closer to him. Mona was relentless, the squeals were frightful and it kept getting louder and louder each time Dua pulled the leash.

Dua began singing, a scare aid technique he developed during childhood. Miraculously it worked, Mona's deafening squeals were replaced with grunts, the rope started to loosen up around Dua's wrist as the animal relaxed the tension and slowly walked towards him.

Dua continued singing courageously as he drew himself towards Mona with the leash. With each step nearing Mona, the leash shortened in length, the loose ends were firmly tied around the length of his arm. The gruelling task now was how to calm Mona down and bring the animal up the mountain.

Dua was in a predicament, but without thinking he took a deep breath, bent down and tightly clasped the struggling animal around the belly with both arms as he switched his footing and mounted the sixty five kilogram pig up on his right shoulder. He then quickly positioned the pig across his shoulder like a yoke, struggling to stand upright.

Dua tightly grabbed the two front hoofs with his right fist, and the two back hoofs with his left fist and he started walking immediately. He paid no attention to Mona's deafening squeals. The first few strides were brisk, Dua wished he could maintain the same momentum all the way up to the house, but experience had taught him that this much weight will wear him down along the way.

The fear that Dua was fighting to hold down was now suppressed by the weight of the animal on his shoulders. He looked down and focused on the path, occasionally adjusting the animal on his shoulders firmly. He didn't look up to the summit, something he had thought of himself; if the road is far you must not see or even think about the distance, focus on a single step at a time, eventually you will be surprised that you are already there before you know it. Works all the time.

Mona's struggle slowed down, the deafening squeals were replaced with calm grunting which Dua responded with his own grunts as if chatting with the animal on his shoulders.

Dua continued the same hasty climb up the mountain without catching his breath; there is plenty of rest at the top, now is certainly not the time or the place, Dua thought.

Dua used a lot of energy reserve this time; carefully positioning his footing firmly before allowing his whole body weight including that of Mona to mount pressure while he maneuvered the next footing, he will be continuing the same process all the way home if he can manage it.

The distance up ahead was blocked out from his mind, every step he took, the further he got away from Waghi. Away from the riverside as far as possible. Along the river bank the ghastly figure that had sent Dua into his frightful retreat remained standing and watched as Dua scurried up the summit. A gas lighter flicked. The ghastly figure lit up a cigarette and smoked.

Slowly and quietly, like snakes, venturing out into the open, the darkest parts of the bushes came alive as four other men came forth; darkness itself had taken human form with silhouettes of high-powered rifles. They approached the loner who was standing beside the river bank and stood beside him looking in the same direction without uttering a word. Their faces barely visible. They had been watching Dua in the shadows from the moment Dua came down looking for Mona, and had remained inconspicuous until Dua had left.

"Did you see the way he mounted the pig on his shoulders?" The tallest figure in the group with a raspy Western Highlands accent chuckled. "When I was he's age the only thing I could mount was a woman's leg. I'm guessing he hasn't laid with a woman in a long time." Soft sassy chuckles broke out amongst the men.

"Should we follow him?" asked the Western Highlander again. The others agreed and hummed in harmony. They all seemed to be facing the loner for his approval.

"Not now, let him go," the loner said with a deep authoritative voice. On that note the men slowly dispersed. They walked apart from each other but in the same direction. In a matter of seconds they all disappeared into the night.

Chapter 4

Dua maintained full steam up to about seventy to eighty meters and as he had foreseen, he was totally exhausted, he felt he couldn't go on any further. He stood for a moment to recuperate. Mona hadn't struggled anymore – probably enjoying the comfortable free ride home, or she realised Dua could easily throw her down the cliff if she gave him a hard time.

Dua heard the sound of Waghi River behind him becoming slightly distant, an indication that he had made a fair bit of ground from it, but Dua knew that didn't amount to a thing, there was still a long way to go, he thought.

Alone and weakened, Dua physically felt his back started to ache and his muscles contracted. This was the second time in less than three hours today he had mounted a heavy load up this very mountain, his whole being couldn't take the abuse anymore, but his will, his determination said otherwise.

Dua summoned his strength and journey on up; the flesh was weak but the spirit is willing. The sweat dribbling down his forehead over his nose and onto his lip was snatched by his tongue in a desperate effort to quench his thirst. The saliva in his mouth had dried up, his breathing grew heavier, he felt his whole being quiver, and he was hungry beyond measure. Whatever calorie intake during the day had all been used up – his battery was nearing its lifespan.

At that moment, Dua felt he couldn't go on any further, this time he was certain of it. He let down Mona onto the grass and sat beside her, exhausted, and looking back down at where he had come up from. Staring into nothingness. Darkness had fully engulfed the whole surroundings. Only the distant cry of the river could be heard.

He slowly looked over to his right far off on the other mountain and saw Kundiawa Town with electric lights. Mona started to become agitated. Dua rubbed Mona's head trying to calm the pig down; but Mona grunts as if telling Dua 'we should keep moving'.

Dua animal responded, "I understand you want to go home, I am truly exhausted, cut me some slack, just let me catch my breath first." Mona kept grunting, reminding Dua that there was still a long way to go.

"I can't carry you this time, you are on your own," Dua said, hoping the animal will understand and comply. "Follow me, and don't walk on the left side, you might fall off the cliff and drag me with you." Dua said, reminding himself to grip the leash that was tied around his arm tightly.

Dua got up to his feat sluggishly and summoned Mona to join him, Mona responded slowly leading the way while Dua followed closely behind.

His mind had already reached home awaiting his body to join him. All he could think about now was home, his grandmother's cooking, and his bed. He thought about the mushrooms and the beans that awaited him at the top, his stomach rumbled with complaints.

Dua cursed himself for bringing up the menu at such a time, but in a way the thoughts alone was all the motivation he needed to complete the journey, there was reward at the top for the struggle he was going through. How pleased Grandma would be to see both Dua and Mona in one piece; only her acknowledgement and gratefulness will be sufficient enough to compensate Dua for the burden he accepted.

Dua owed Grandma everything, and he had proven himself time and time again to be a worthy investment. Grandma always reiterates how complicated things would have turned out for her if Dua had never been born. How she would struggle to survive without the help from anyone.

At her age she couldn't possibly live without support, she had derived her youthful zeal from Dua, and Dua never treated her like an old woman. He always spoke to her as he would to his peers, and she would return the same gesture always with youthful flair– the pair were indeed best of friends.

As Dua continued his journey up the distant sound of the river was a constant reminder of what had just transpired. Dua thought of the ghastly figure beside the river and chills ran down his spine.

Mona was advancing much quicker, ever so keen to be getting on home. Dua struggled to keep pace with the animal. He resorted this time to walking on all fours up the steep slopes, and this time Mona was dragging Dua, their roles reversed – Mona was now leading Dua home, and Dua trailed behind on all fours like a pig.

Had someone with a torch light arrived at that instant he or she would be astounded, even terrified. Dua released the rope around his arm bit by bit to lengthen the distance between him and Mona, trying his best not to drag the animal back which might be catastrophic for both of them.

Mona galloped hastily up, her hoofs thumping on the earth.

Without a warning Mona dashed up, the final length of the rope that was still around Dua's arm slid right off forcefully and Dua was yanked forward. He fell awkwardly into the grass.

When Dua got up and realised the rope had disappeared from his hand it was already too late, Mona had ventured off alone into the darkness.

"Damn you!" Dua screamed.

Chapter 5

Dua looked back down at Waghi River, the river was now distant, he felt like he was looking at a strange evil place that would lure him back if he kept on looking. Dua shook his head and continued walking up. He finally reached home, and arrived at the front yard and continued walking around the house grunting. He went to the small pig shed at the back of the house to check hoping Mona somehow let herself in.

He got there, looked down, and saw that Mona was already asleep peacefully inside the shed. Dua sat down beside the shed, collapsed back and groaned heavily with such relief. All of a sudden Dua wasn't hungry or thirsty anymore, and all he wanted to do was sleep on the ground next to the pig shed.

What a day it had been. The sudden eruption of laughter coming from inside the house snapped Dua back to earth. He quickly got to his feet. Fully alert. "What the? Who is inside the house with my grandmother" he thought. Dua stood quietly for a moment and tried to listen carefully.

Having company at any given time up here is odd. They never get any visitors here. This is strange.

Dua walked over towards the cane stalk wall and slowly placed his right ear on the wall and tried to make out who was inside the house. Dua could hear a man talking indistinctly, barely audible, so that Dua couldn't establish his voice, he could only hear his grandmother's loudmouth laughing occasionally. Dua stood perplexed.

Again, Dua placed his right ear on the wall to listen. As Dua listened, he could hear his grandmother talking now. Discreetly. "I discovered the feeble infant crying for two days," Grandma said. "Had I arrived a day later the poor thing would have been dead. I'm a mother after all, I was weak. But of course, I do regret going there, I should have just let the pathetic creature cry to death." Laughter erupted again.

Dua was instantly taken aback, he couldn't believe what he was hearing. Dua reversed back and looked around in case he had climbed up the wrong mountain and ended up at another house. What the hell is going on?

Dua marched around the house and pushed the door wide open. He stood at the door, puzzled after realising who Grandma was talking with.

"Inspector?" Dua thought out aloud.

"Ah, Dua! You finally showed up." The Inspector beamed from behind the furnace, his skull stood out from the dark hollow shadows on his bony face. Dua somehow felt like a guest in his own house, the overpowering personality of Inspector Ialasam Gelma had a similar effect on everyone in the community.

Dua remained standing with no intention of sitting down. The Inspector noticed Dua's obvious nervous reaction. "I think you should sit down Dua. I wouldn't have come up here if it wasn't important." Said the Inspector.

"I'm fine thank you, I think I'll stand."

"Is that so?" The Inspector sighed under his breath. Disappointed. He looked up at Dua steadily while slipping his right hand inside his jacket, Dua looked on attentively.

Dua's heart immediately sank when the Inspector drew out his pistol and held it out in his right hand. Dua withdrew back and looked at Grandma. Grandma sat motionless. Dua struggled to speak.

"Dua, I think you should sit down." Said Grandma, quietly.

"I think you should listen to your grandmother Dua. The gun in my hand has taken four human lives already, there are nine bullets in this gun, I still haven't used five bullets yet," the Ialasam Gelma concurred.

Right about now sitting down seem like a damn good idea. Dua sat down exactly where he stood. I have done nothing wrong, I shouldn't cower from this man, Dua thought.

The Inspector kept his piercing gaze, "Listen Dua, I came here to tell you that a group of men are on the run from the police," said the Ialasam. "They are armed and extremely dangerous. For the past few weeks they have been responsible for every major crime along the highway."

"I hear you," said Dua, uneasily.

"Good. You see, no one knows exactly who these men are, no one. Maybe they do, but are afraid to say it."

"If you are asking if I know something, I can honestly say that I don't know a thing."

"Who says I was asking if you know something?"

"Well I just assume –"

"Don't assume! I hate people who assume."

"Boss I'm sorry –"

"What are you sorry about Dua? Do you know something?"

"Of course not."

"Then you shut up and listen carefully before you talk."

Dua nodded in obedience, but he couldn't focus especially when Ialasam Gelma still had the silver revolver swinging around in his hand. Minus that gun and Dua could think of all the possible ways he would attack Ialasam, probably throw him off the cliff and make it look like an accident.

"Open your ears and listen very carefully Dua," said the Ialasam. "I am in pursuit of these men. I can feel I am really close. My gut tells me they are hiding somewhere here."

The ghastly figure beside Waghi River! Dua thought.

"Is there something you are holding back?" Asked Ialasam.

"No, I'm not," Dua said. "I haven't seen anyone around here in a very long time. If the robbers are around here somewhere I wouldn't know, there are many secret routes and hideouts that were used during tribal fights, they could be anywhere –"

"If you know something and you are covering up for these criminals you will be held accountable as an accomplice."

"I don't know anything right now. But I can promise you that if I see something out of the ordinary, I will come and see you personally."

"I appreciate that Dua. We need to work together on this."

"I really hope you catch these bandits."

"And why is that?"

"Because they are bad men."

"Because they are bad men?"

"Yeah –"

"You sound like a pregnant woman when you say that. They are not bad men, they are opportunists! I'm a bad man! Our paths haven't crossed yet. Anyways, why are you all alone here? Why don't you go stay with family in Lae or somewhere? It looks very lonely and boring here."

"I'm alone, I'm not lonely."

"Fair enough."

"My grandmother is the only thing keeping me here. She has only few years to live. Can't leave her alone."

"I can see that."

"Thank you."

"Look Dua, I am trying my best to be nice here. But, if I find out you are hiding something from me. I am going to come back and burn you alive inside this house. Do you understand?"

Dua nodded without saying anything. Ialasam's demeanour seemed to be the product of an icy divorce from his inner spirit. A troubled childhood perhaps? Dua thought.

"The world of crime is an illusion," said the Ialasam. "I hope you do not condemn yourself and run when all the puzzle comes together and I find out you are the missing piece."

"I am not running. I have nothing to hide." Dua said firmly.

"Very well. I apologise for the manner in which I have conducted myself. But I can never be too certain."

Dua lifted his head and looked at Ialasam, "you are a good police man Ialasam. I mean it."

"That's high praise Dua. But you and I both know you are just saying this because you feel intimidated by the man with the gun in this room."

Dua suddenly felt awkward, the thought of going back down to Waghi and introduce himself to the ghastly figure he had just ran away from seemed like a good idea right about now.

Ialasam chuckled, "Grandma, come sit beside me. You have been awfully quiet, I would love to hear your thoughts."

Dua eyed his grandmother, don't you dare – Grandma purred as she reluctantly moved closer to Ialasam.

"You should hide that gun Ialasam, I don't like guns." Grandma said, ruefully.

"Most certainly, but have you held a gun before?"

"Me! God forbid no. I couldn't even pass my late husband's bow during tribal fights, I discourage all form of weapons, especially guns. I think people are better off without them."

"I admire the way you think. If everyone thinks the same way as you, there will be no reason for me to carry one."

"But you are a Police Officer, it is your duty to bare one," said Grandma.

"Thank you. Can I ask you a favor?"

"Of course my dear."

"Nothing will thrill me more right now if you would be so kind as to hold my gun in your hand for a brief moment."

Dua felt uncomfortable with that suggestion, he leaned back uneasily as Grandma reached over without hesitation and grasped the revolver inside both her hands. Dua was now more alarmed seeing the pistol in the hands of his grandmother after Ialasam just seconds ago. But then Ialasam seemed ecstatic.

Dua saw that Ialasam's idea of fun was dangerously out of order. Grandma seemed distant. She held the gun closely to her face the way she would when looking for lice on Mona's back; scanning it carefully. Dua was tempted to ask whether she was looking for lice on the gun. Grandma slowly looked up at Ialasam and raised the gun. It took a while for Dua to register that Grandma wasn't giving the pistol back to Ialasam, she was aiming the pistol at Ialasam.

Dua couldn't process what he was seeing. He shrieked, "Grandma! What are you doing?"

"Shut up Dua! This man comes into our house and show us no respect; I will kill him right here."

Dua gasped for air. Ialasam kept looking at Grandma without flinching.

"So you think you can come here and push us around? Speak now!"

"I truly admire your courage Grandma. Dua is very lucky to have you, I wish I knew you better," Ialasam said.

"Go to hell you devil!" Grandma screamed and pulled the trigger. Nothing. She repeatedly squeezed the trigger, but nothing.

Ialasam isn't moved. He seemed amused. He reached over and gently retrieved the gun. "Oh, I forgot to tell you," Ialasam said. "The safety is on. Maybe next time Grandma." Ialasam stood up and kissed Grandma on her forehead before exiting the house.

Just like that.

Dua sat there mortified, he could not believe what he had just witnessed. After a brief moment Dua stood up and exited the hamlet without a word. Outside, under the moonlight he saw Ialasam heading down towards the direction of Wara Simbu. Dua kept watching as Ialasam kept heading down and disappeared. Dua followed right after him.

Chapter 6

Four kilometers away at the Kundiawa Police Station, the Chimbu Provincial Commander or PPC Kombri Gigma, a tall lean man in his late fifties, with teary eyes, stood inside his office talking on the telephone.

That night the PPC was not in a good mood. His tone over the telephone did not correspond with his agitated expressions. Whoever was on the line must have been important otherwise, knowing the PPC, he would have already slammed the telephone down.

"I – I understand," the PPC said. "But, given the scope of our operations we are working well within our means, the resources and budget we have at hand are all being fully utilised even exhausted to a certain extent, it wasn't meant for –"

The PPC was cut off by the person from the other line before he could complete his sentence. He ground his teeth and clenched his left knuckles in sequence, a sign to those who are well acquainted with him that the man does not tolerate interruptions when he speaks.

"Look," the PPC said, firmly. "We need a well-coordinated effort and the support of the national government to curb this disease of lawlessness in the province, I understand how vital this policy is however my numerous –"

The PPC was again interrupted for the second time. This time by the knock on his door. He pardoned the person on the other line, held the telephone to his chest and blurted a curse to whoever it was on the other side of the door to enter.

A short stubby police officer in uniform materialised with an anxious look on his face. The PPC signalled the officer with a hand gesture to take a seat at the front desk before continuing his dialogue on the telephone.

The PPC sincerely apologised to the person on the other line who must have overheard the curse. The stubby police officer, now seated, looked to be in his early thirties with a kind of face you could easily recognise from a baby photo. The wooden chair squeaked when he stretched his legs out comfortably resting his thick hands over his belly, and relaxed with an air of ease other right-minded officers in his rank couldn't have done.

The PPC glanced over and became slightly annoyed. As the Provincial Police boss continued talking on the telephone, the officer let his eyes wonder around the room. Everything about this office was well organised; from the aroma of coffee beans to the order of stationaries on the front desk. The Royal Papua New Guinea Constabulary Seal (RPNGC) was crafted on all the wooden chair arm rests and backs, the filing cabinet had files and books arranged with librarian precision, the wall proudly boasted awards and portraits of the PPC's life achievements that the officer now seated could only marvel at.

Photos of the PPC's colourful courier as a young police officer up to more recent foreign dignitaries. The stubby images of him dining with state ministers an officer suddenly felt smaller for obvious reasons. He felt a gaze and turned to catch his boss frowning at him.

"What do you want?" PPC Kombri Gigma said, as he carefully placed the telephone down and relaxed back in his revolving chair. The stubby officer felt uneasy,

"Sorry to barge in like that Sir, I –"

"Don't worry about it James," said the PPC. "I just got off the telephone with the Governor. The good Governor in all his wisdom thinks we should be concentrating more on Community Policing to curb lawlessness in this province. It insults me personally when he fails to realise that I have been doing that long before he could grasp that concept. How do they expect results from us without their commitment?"

Everyone in the department understood how adamant the PPC is with regards to Community Policing. James fell silent as if his boss had intended him to answer that question on behalf of the Provincial Government. The PPC continued; sitting sideways, resting his right arm on the desk, "these politicians are merely transitory figureheads who pass fleetingly across the chessboard. Men like me have been around long enough to understand the game with some perspective," said the PPC. "Being just an MP is not nearly enough to comprehend the true complexities of police work in Papua New Guinea. The crimes along the highway have gone from bad to worse. We are in a state of emergency. I am going to resign, I can't deal with this pressure."

James quickly searched his boss's face for any glint of humour.

"So tell me James," Asked the PPC, frankly. "Why have you come here if not to offer similar sentiment? Or did you come here to share one of your lame jokes?"

"S – sir." James said, reluctantly. "There has been another highway robbery."

His boss sighed deeply, "Did we apprehend any suspects?"

"No, not yet sir. The robbery must have occurred over an hour ago, we were only informed of this thirty minutes ago, by the time the highway patrol had arrived at the scene the criminals were long gone."

"How was this robbery executed?"

"It was carried out in the same way as the six other previous robberies; they didn't search the old ladies, but everyone else on-board including children were searched and robbed. We believe it's the same gang sir."

"Of course it's the same gang you idiot. Where are the victims now?"

"They are all outside in the carpark," James said, uncertain. "We are trying to interview them one by one. One of the passengers from Mount Hagen claims he recognised one of the robber's voice."

"How certain is he?"

"He said he's very certain. He also claims to know the robber personally."

The Station Commander immediately got to his feet and walked towards the door. James followed his boss, struggling to keep pace.

Chapter 7

"What happened Apa? Could you explain the events to the best of your memory?" PPC Kombri Gigma asked.

The victim; a serious looking man with an excessive beard sat at the other end of the wooden desk facing the PPC inside the small questioning room. Three other police men including Constable James Balkan stood around. The officers kept their hair cropped in a buzz cut, giving them an air of military command.

"We were ambushed, they came out of nowhere while we were slowly going up the slope at Talis," said Apa. "They hid behind the bushes by the roundabout, when we curved in they jump right at us before we knew it. They robbed everyone, one of the robbers even snatched a batman figure from this kid. But they didn't lay a single finger on the two old women on board."

"Can you remember how many they were?" Kombri asked.

"Yeah, there were five of them I think, three of them robbed us while the other two stood on lookout. They were all wearing masks so I couldn't see their faces, they all had very high powered guns, I noticed two of them had AK47s."

"How did you know it was an AK47?"

"I used to have one. But I gave it away to my cousin brother, he needed it more than I did." Apa answered, frankly.

The Station Commander leaned back, he needed a moment to let the audacity of Apa's honesty to settle in. The line between right and wrong is wearing thin by the minute, Kombri thought.

"So, you can clearly recognise one of the robbers' voices?" Kombri asked,

"Yes, I recognised one of the robbers' voices, I also know who he is, his name is Kembol."

"Pardon me?"

"His name is Kembol, he's from Dei Council. I know that for certain. We call him Dei Kembol."

"And you can confirm all this, just by voice recognition?"

"Yes. I am familiar with his voice, we are both from the same place it is not such a thing I would lie about especially under these circumstances," said Apa, firmly.

"It could be someone else, all Western Highlanders have the same accent, couldn't you have mistaken?"

"All of you Chimbus have the same accent but I'm sure you can easily differentiate one another between yourselves. I couldn't have been wrong, because when I called out his name – he froze briefly before he took off."

"How do you know him?"

"Everyone knows him. He is a trouble maker."

"I see." Said PPC Kombri, thoughtfully.

"I hope you catch him. We really don't need this kind of man in our community."

A buzz erupted inside the small questioning room. "Kembol?" The PPC did a double-take, "I think I know this guy. I heard he was in prison."

"That's what I thought too. Until tonight. But, why?" Said Apa.

PPC Kombri stared at him, "what do you mean?"

"Why would our own people do this?"

"Easy money, that's why," Kombri said, plainly. "Your tribesman links up with the local gang here, supplies them with information regarding your people's highway business trips. That's why all the highway robberies are done to Highland owned vehicles exclusively."

"That's messed up. My people back home are thinking your people are doing this. But it's our own."

"Criminals are affiliated with each other, that's what makes their movement fluid," said Kombri. "Oddly enough it is deemed a moral convenience to raise hell outside of their community, in that way they still get along with the community under the impression that they are innocent." The room fell silent momentarily.

PPC Kombri Gigma sighed, "I have to make a phone call, James you take over." The PPC stood up, his mobile phone was already inside his bony hands, he glanced through his contacts and made a call, as the call went through he pressed the mobile phone against his right ear and exited the questioning room.

Constable James sat at the chair previously occupied by the PPC and cleared his throat, "Well Apa, it looks like you have given us a lot of valuable information tonight, you have had a rough night I won't take your time much longer. I am to write a witness statement on this paper. Can you write?"

"Yeah, I can write. I completed grade twelve."

"Good for you. I will leave you to it. Will be back to check on you. Be plain and simple when you express." Apa faked a smile and he started to write. James stood up and motioned his colleagues to exit the room as well.

Chapter 8

The Horizon's Lae based editor Gilbert Gigma was just turning off the lights in his Lae office when his phone rang. He had no intention of picking up at this hour—that is, until he glimpsed the caller-ID display.

"Hey uncle, what's up?" Gilbert asked.

"Gilbert." The PPC Kombri Gigma's voice sounded anxious. "Thank God you're here. I need your help."

Gilbert sighed heavily. "What do you need?"

"Alright listen, I need information. Last month if I recall correctly you ran a story on Boimo prison break out?"

Gilbert frowned. "Yeah."

"Have all the escapees been recaptured?"

"No. Six of them are still at large, the police only managed to recapture seven of the escapees, unfortunately three of them were shot dead."

"Do you have the names of the escapees that are still at large?"

Gilbert scratched the tip of his nose. "Yeah, I think I do have it, the information is somewhere here. There are papers all over the place."

"Gilbert, can you try to be organised in your life? It's actually good for your health son."

"Uncle, I am a very unorganised organised person, things may be all over the place but I know exactly where they are."

"Alright, not every branch on a tree has the same shape."

"What?"

"Never mind just fax me the information as soon as you can."

"I'm looking now," Gilbert said. "Oh snap! I have it all inside my computer, I'm going to email it to you."

"Yeah that will do just fine, send it right now."

Gilbert sensed the urgency in his uncle's voice. "It's not so often a PPC does the investigative duties, it's good to see you haven't lost all that spark." His computer pinged. "Okay, hold on….this may take a while." He moused through the folders on his screen. "You can hang-up, I will send it."

"Thanks, Gilbert," Kombri Gigma said, sounding grateful. "I owe you one."

"You owe me a drink—". The line went dead. Gilbert stared at the receiver and shook his head.

PPC Kombri Gigma returned back to his office, and sat in front of his Acer desk computer, waiting for his kind nephew to email him the information regarding the identity of all the Boimo Prison escapees that are still at large. It had been almost over fifteen minutes and still there was no email from his nephew yet.

As Kombri sat alone, absently gazing around, the silence of his office was interupted by the ring of his fax machine. What's taking that idiot so long? Wearily, he reached over to retrieve the fax. The incoming fax lay in the tray. Sighing, he scooped up the papers and looked at it. Instantly, his mood shifted. The image on the first page was that of Kembol.

Kembol had used an alias when he was arrested in Lae and sent to Prison, it was only after he had escaped that they figured out who he really was.

Kombri quickly flipped to the next page with exhilarating interest. On the next page he was staring at the face of two very much similar looking men – anyone would guess they were related by their striking resemblance.

Kombri Gigma flipped to the third and final page and stared at the image before him. He set a moment gathering his thoughts. All the pieces of the puzzle came together at that moment.

His eyes were drawn this time to the blinking red light on his fax machine. Whoever had sent this fax was still on the line . . . waiting to talk. Kombri gazed at the blinking light a long time. Then, sighing, he picked up the receiver.

"I had to print it and fax them to you, sorry it took a while," the familiar voice of his nephew said when he answered the line.

"I thought you were going to email me?"

"Yeah me too –"

"It's alright, thanks son."

"Uncle why the interest in a bunch of escapees in Lae?" His nephews voice rigid, mechanical. "I am a reporter after all..... curiosity gets the best of me."

Kombri looked at the fax machine, annoyed. Curiosity also killed the cat. "They are all here," Kombri said. "All the escapees. All five of them are here in Chimbu."

"Oh my. No wonder the crime up there has soared."

"Is there anything I should know about these men?"

"Yes. There is something you should know. All of them were arrested in front of Bank South Pacific Lae nine months ago from a tip off."

"How are they out?"

"Beats me."

"Were the insiders identified?"

"Yeah, after they arrested the gang one of the security guards disappeared without a trace, it was actually sad because he must have thought the gang would sell him out which never happened. It doesn't make much difference now."

"That's heartbreaking. Keep going."

"Well, they were armed to the teeth when the police swiftly seized them inside a dark Kiejeng. They probably intended to conceal their weapons and waltz inside the bank. Luckily there was no motivation for a gun fight, otherwise if the gang had pulled off the robbery it would have been a blood bath."

"So they are here to finish what they started off in Lae."

"Uncle, why Kundiawa? It's a small town."

"I know. I mean no one is stupid enough to rob a bank here, it has never been done before because it is impossible; one way in, no way out, even if they did it will be a bad idea. That's why they are holding up MPV busses."

"Uncle, these men are all about bad ideas. You can never be too certain. Every fools the next, and it grows in proportion."

"Six similar highway holdups doesn't seem much of a growth in proportion. Anyways, I'll talk to you later son."

"No worries Chief, and when are —" Kombri ended the call immediately. His nephew had the tendency of coming up with all sorts of silly requests. Kombri was not in the mood for that.

Chapter 10

A burly, square-chested man with a chiselled face by the name of Nem was the Station Commander in Kundiawa. He spent the majority of his time coordinating his army of para military police officers or the mobile squads ensuring the Chimbu section of the Okuk Highway stayed trouble free. Tonight, had been a busy night at the station, but Nem had his own problems. Nem was still troubled by the report he received that afternoon from the Day High School's Principle concerning his daughter.

His daughter got into a nasty fight with another female student over a boy, Nem's daughter nearly gouged out the other contestant's eye. Nem was up to his neck with problems, finding another school for his daughter would be an extra burden, he was bombarded with workloads as a result of the increased crimes along the highway, the last thing he needed was a personal setback.

Nem's mind drifted off as he stood beside the front counter vaguely glancing through the daily paper when the PPC approached him from behind, "Commander?" Nem immediately turned around.

"You got minute?" Said the PPC. "Need to talk.

"Nem folded the newspaper and briskly followed the Station Commander who led him outside the car park. When the PPC summoned Nem it had to be grave. Kombri often referred to Nem and his crew as the 'force of execution', a manner of speech many found ugly and cold. Disconcerting.

When the PPC finally stopped walking, they were both standing in front of the PPC Kombri's parked silver Prado. Kombri leaned against his Prado and spoke discreetly to Nem in all seriousness, Nem inched closer and listened attentively. Nem didn't ask questions nor did he interrupt, it was one of his attributes that Kombri admired, Nem was a man of few words and more action.

"After twelve minutes of listening to Kombri talk, Nem finally gave a knowing "Alright, I will handle this." Nem said only five words with an air of finality and walked off.

An officer who looked to be in his early twenties claimed the front seat of the RPNGC vehicle, sky blue Toyota Land Cruiser comfortably. Nem arrived beside the door. "Get the hell out of my seat and go seat at the back son."

The young officer apologised sincerely and quickly did as he was told. Five other officers sitting at the back including the driver laughed out loud. Nem wasn't even smiling. What he had just heard from PPC Kombri was no laughing matter. The young officer hopped in the back, pulled the door shut and sat quietly. Nem glanced back and saw six astute police men sitting behind him. Wonderful.

"Go east." Nem instructed the driver. The ten-seater Toyota Land Cruiser slowly pulled out from the station, eased onto the main road and screamed past Yuwai Market like a jet fighter on the runway. Late night vendors and drunkards quickly looked down or turned away whenever Nem looked out, as if staring at a police officer is a punishable offence, which ironically was more likely to happen. Nem lit up a monster brus and thought of what he had just learnt from Kombri as the Cruiser descended down Prenorokwa Hill.

Chapter 11

Wara Simbu is about a kilometer down from Kundiawa Town. It is famous for its entertainment and leisure activities all year around. Night time in Wara Simbu meant people from everywhere gathered around to sell, drink and gamble, the routine was the same every night.

The locals find daylight less convenient to engage in activities that only the cover of darkness can grant its full potential.

That night, like every other night, Thomas Grakumne, a forty-eight years old alcoholic stood in front of his liquor shop at the western end of the Wara Simbu Bridge; drinking his beer and watching drunken brawls. Thomas's pleasant mood was replaced with a grin when he saw this particular young woman gleefully conversing with a tipsy young man. Thomas felt uneasy watching the two young, apparently attracted to each other talking and smiling, noticeably flirting.

Thomas shouted over. The young woman turned around instantly recognising Thomas's voice with an alarmed look on her face. She rudely gestured regretfully at the young man whom she was talking with and walked over to Thomas. She was attractive, in her early twenties, her curvy feminine structure from a distance was unmistakable, even more so too defined. Thomas felt irritated at the gauntlet of drunken lustful male eyes following her.

"Hay baby," one man called over. "Nice butt."

"Nice try," she replied flatly.

"I wouldn't mind being your second husband."

She rolled her eyes and kept walking: men!! Thomas waited. When she came near Thomas stepped forward.

"Susan who is that man you were talking with?".

Susan stopped dead, "He was my classmate back in high school."

Thomas asked "You seem to have a lot to discuss," said Thomas. "What were you discussing?"

"What does it matter? We were just talking."

"What were you talking about?"

"My God Thomas. He asked me how I was doing and I told him that I'm d –"

"He asked if you are married? That's none of his business!"

"Thomas, you are going to make a scene."

"What's his name?"

"His name? Ah hmm his name's Kua." Replied Susan, reluctantly.

"I'm going over to talk to your boyfriend Kua."

Susan struggled to maintain her stance. "Don't do this. Please. It's embarrassing."

"I know you Susan. You would have gotten in the car with him and took off if I was not here. Am I right or wrong?"

"Thomas stop it, please."

"Am I right or wrong?" Susan shook her head in disbelief. "I am done trying to stop you," said Thomas. "You can do whatever you desire. If I wanted to fight with all your boyfriends, I'd be fighting every guy in Chimbu."

"You are drunk Thomas. We should go home now."

"No! I am not going home!" Thomas said heatedly. "You are screwing everyone here! I am not taking you home! You can go over to that guy! Just piss off!" The words came out loud, his voice hanging naked in an ill-timed lull. Vendors nearby glanced over.

"You are humiliating me you drunk useless old man," Susan said with glistening eyes.

"Oh. So I'm old and useless ah?" Susan felt her defenses melt away. Thomas swung the half empty beer bottle at Susan, and Susan screamed and ducked! In fearful desperation Susan ran behind a skinny drug addict by the name Wemin who unfortunately stood there. Wemin knew about Thomas's uncontrollable rages and violent nature, he was more terrified than Susan.

In defence of both, Wemin pleaded with both hands stretched forward – Thomas's powerful hands seized Wemin's wrist and yanked him forward. Wemin felt himself being spun around. Before Wemin could even process what was happening, a rock-hard fist collided with his sternum. The poor guy crumpled to the dirt groaning in pain as Thomas's large black form stepped away from him.

Thomas savagely looked around at every other man who stood around, anyone else? They all withdrew back. Thomas turned his attention towards Susan again. Nobody wanted any part of it. Susan was on her own.

Susan made quick haste towards the road. She almost came into collusion with a packed Toyota Land Cruiser with an open back. The people on the car shouted at her, she went around and ran looking over her shoulder with panic and fear sweeping across her face. The people who gathered and watched mumbled at each other.

An elderly woman who had just arrived screamed at them, "Can you men do something! He is going to kill her!"

"That's not our problem. I would have done the same thing if I was Thomas," one man defended. "Thomas already paid her bride price! She has no right to look at another man! We will not tolerate a woman who has no respect for our brother!" Another added.

"That's a poor excuse of you men!" The elderly women snapped. "Imagine if that was your daughter or sister, are you all going to stand there and watch? You are all bunch of cowards!"

"Shut up all of you!" Wemin cried out. "Where the hell is the guy Susan was talking with? If it wasn't for him none of this would have ever happened! Where is that guy? It's all his fault!"

Those who had just arrived at the scene looked at each other confused. Nearby vendors who had witnessed everything remained silent, except – "He's over there!" Someone pointed, "Susan's boyfriend is over there! It's all his fault!"

Everyone turned to face that direction. Before anything else could be said Wemin walked out from the group followed by two others. The men snaked towards Kua like three hyenas that have just spotted easy meal. Kua could see all the fuss that was going on in front of Thomas's liquor shop from where he was standing. Other men ostensibly who are with Kua figured it wasn't such a good idea to hang around there anymore.

"Kua we need to go," one of them said. "This does not look good."

"Stop being a wuss," Kua said. "Half of these people are related to me, I'm not afraid of them".

"Well, that's just reassuring Kua, what about us?" Another said. "We came here to drink, not to find love."

"Nothing is going to happen," said Kua, "I will talk to them –"

"Nothing is going to happen? Are you blind? Look over there. It's already building and it's about to get worse." They could see Wemin and the two men heading directly towards them, and acting fast.

Kua motioned his friends to sit down, "let me talk to them." Kua stepped out from his friends and greeted the men before they came near. "Goodnight to you."

"Shut up!" Wemin barked. "Why were you talking to that married women?"

"I didn't know she was married."

"If it wasn't for you Thomas wouldn't have attacked me!"

"I am sorry."

"Save your sorry! We are going to teach you a lesson!"

"What are you going to do?"

"We are going to fu–" Wemin caught a straight shot unexpectedly to his mouth he swallowed the last bit of his sentence along with a tooth. Wemin was knocked out cold before his body lay flat on the earth. The two men beside Wemin viciously charged at Kua.

Kua's friends joined in the fight. The traffic came to a halt as the fight intensified and spilled onto the main road. They fought like dogs. The gruesome barbarity of the battle without sanity and remorse brought to light the dark savage nature of man. It was as if beneath every man's skin was an animal just waiting for an opportunity to be unleashed.

The whole traffic on the highway from both the east and the west came to an abrupt halt. Cars that were already within the fighting zone made quick desperate detours amidst all forms of missiles heading their way. Observers gathering fervently beside liquor shops and within the safety of their fence held their breaths as they watched the pandemonium before them. From the western end of the highway people saw a police car charging in. From the front seat of the standard RPNGC Government issued Toyota Land Cruiser Commander Nem could see a very ugly fight right in the middle of the Okuk Highway.

"Drive into the fight, run over one or two if you must!" Nem ordered. The driver complied without hesitation. The six officers at the back cocked their guns. The Police vehicle stormed the party full speed with sirens, gunshots, and the chilling red and blue lights up top, sending almost everyone scampering into the nearby coffee gardens.

In a matter of minutes the roadside was almost completely empty. Except for Kua, his friends, and a few unfortunate men who still lay flat on their backs. Kua watched as the police car rolled towards him like a terrifying beast. One hell of an entrance, Kua thought. Kua was relieved to see the police.

Nem instructed the driver to park beside Kua. Both doors at the back of the Cruiser opened at the same time, and the six officers jumped out. Nem remained seated.

"Did you knock out all three of them?" Nem asked. "Yes, yes I did boss." Nem looked impressed. But he wasn't happy. "What is the matter with you eh!" Nem screamed. "What happened here?"

"I didn't start the fight."

"I don't care!"

"You have to believe me, you can ask anyone here, they all saw who started the fight."

"Shut that hole in your face," Nem said angrily. "Do you think anyone here gives a damn!" Kua realized Nem had a point. The locals worked as a single unit; it is highly unlikely someone would stand in Kua's defence.

People started to gather.

Chapter 12

Susan ran directly into someone's chest while she was frantically looking over her shoulder. A powerful hand swooped her back in before she fell. With teary eyes she lifted her head and locked her gaze with Dua. Dua looked down at her, completely immobile.

Thomas came to an abrupt halt at the sight of Dua. Under the moonlit sky Susan noticed something utterly strange in Thomas's reaction. Thomas was afraid of Dua. Both men looked at each other, the intensity could be felt yet Susan couldn't place what it was. Susan realised a fight between the two men seemed imminent, yet for some strange reason neither one of them had the audacity.

"Dua. Hand her over." Thomas said, finally. There were many things Dua could have said to ease the tension, but Dua chose silence. "Dua, this has nothing to do with you. Just hand me that bitch and we call it a bight."

"What did she do?"

"That's none of your business!"

"You tell me what she did."

"You really want to test me?"

"Thomas, she's a defenceless woman. Look at yourself."

Thomas fumed, "I am going to run you over if you do not let her go."

"Try me." Dua said, derisively.

Thomas opened his mouth to speak but nothing came out. Dua's fearless remark reminded Thomas of the age gap. It would be wise to think this through. A small group of people from the roadside started to arrive at the scene, but in less than five seconds they all disappeared after Thomas threatened to burn down their houses. Thomas tried to speak but stopped when the unmistakable sound of an M16 pierced the moonlit sky.

The threesome abruptly turned towards where the shots were fired. Their snags momentarily forgotten. A group of teenagers ran past them towards the road, heading towards where the shots were fired. One would think people normally run away from gunshots but in Papua New Guinea it is the other way around.

"The police must have shot someone!" One of the teenagers called out. "I hope they shot my dad!" Another added.

Thomas gave a final look at Dua and Susan, this isn't over, and followed the teenagers towards the main highway. After Thomas went out of sight, Susan emerged from behind Dua and sigh with a mixture of frustration and relief.

"What a useless man," Susan said. "He only knows how to get drunk and hit woman."

Dua didn't respond to Susan, he had nothing to add on to what Susan had just said.

"I'm sorry I had to drag you into this," Susan said. "God knows what that monster would have done to me if you hadn't shown up."

"What happened?" Dua asked. Susan heaved a heavy sigh and told Dua the whole story from the top. While Susan was still talking; moving her hands and doing all sorts of hypnotic feminine gestures Dua couldn't help but realise Thomas had a perfectly good reason to be paranoid.

A farmer who plants his corn by the roadside and Thomas both had the same problem, Dua thought. Susan paused from talking after noticing Dua's eyes running all over her body.

Susan snapped her fingers, "Hey, are you listening?"

"I am. Please continue." Dua said, slightly embarrassed.

"Anyways," Susan continued. "I wouldn't have married that asshole if I knew the kind of man he is. I have had it up to my neck already."

"Why don't you just leave him? You are still young; you can go anywhere you want."

"It's easier said than done."

"Anything can be done."

"And go where? Like follow you up to lonely mountain?"

"No no no, that's not what I meant –"

"It's alright, I know what you mean." Susan giggled. For some reason Dua found Susan's vulnerability a powerful force enough to move him."

"Dua," Susan said, "I can't go home and face Thomas, you heard what he said, I need to go somewhere else and sleep tonight."

"Susan, that will only make matters worse."

"And what do you suggest I do?"

"I don't know. Wait till he falls asleep before you go home."

"Thomas does not sleep."

"Go to his sister's place then."

"I hate his sisters! I'm not staying here tonight. I'm going to hitchhike a ride back to Kerowagi tonight. You can tell Thomas to come and get me there if he is man enough."

"Alright, listen. If you don't go home Thomas will put the blame on me. I don't want problems."

"Then take me home with you. Who's going to find out?"

"I really want to. But not right now."

"You are a sweetheart Dua." Susan came closer and hugged Dua.

Dua felt his chest muscle tightened. Dua couldn't refuse the scent of her perfume and her warmth. He thought of stopping her but he didn't. Dua reluctantly shrouded his broad arms around her and he somehow felt peace for the first time tonight.

Susan looked up at Dua. Dua fought the temptation to kiss her. Her big brown eyes glimmered in the moonlight, her mouth opened.

"Dua?" She asked, candidly, "are you seriously getting an erection right now?"

Dua shoved Susan away! Susan laughed for the first time that night. How is that even funny? Dua thought. She made matters worse.

Dua turned and immediately walked away from Susan feeling betrayed by his own physical response .

Chapter 13

Thomas Grakumne proceeded insouciantly towards the police headlights wearing a concerned good citizen's face; a face which he had polished over years of practice. As he drew near a crowd of at least forty people, he noticed Commander Nem towering over the crowd, taking mental notes of witness statements.

Nem paused at the sight of Thomas amongst the dozen heads. He pardoned everyone and motioned Thomas over. Thomas outshone everyone, as he does, so effortlessly.

"Thomas!" Nem said. "Such beautiful night to be ruined by few don't you reckon?"

"Don't mention it, these people don't know how to appreciate a good weather like you and I, most of these wild pigs belong up in the forest in their natural habitat, the roadside is meant for civilised men and women." Thomas said, loudly.

"I agree with you Thomas. Beer isn't meant for us."

"The Governor should put a beer ban in Chimbu!"

"But you run a beer shop Thomas."

"I can survive without beer. I only want what's best for the community." A sea of inquisitive stares looked on.

The loudmouthed elderly woman who had protested on behalf of Susan earlier on kept silent and looked on with disgust. As if she couldn't stomach the show Thomas was putting. She fished in her small plastic bag, produced a scone and gorged on it savagely.

"From what I gathered, you and your wife had a fight that lead to all this." Nem said.

"I did have a slight argument with my wife, nothing serious. I don't see how any of this should concern me. This fight is obviously beer politics as usual, I wasn't even aware of it until I heard the gunshots."

"May I ask why you and your wife were arguing?"

"You know how woman are, they just can't stand us looking at other women." The elderly woman practically choked on her scone. She wanted to protest but realised the trouble she'd be in once the police left.

"Where is your wife at the moment?" Nem asked.

"She was right behind me," Thomas gave a show of looking around. "I think she must have gone home. I'll send someone to look for her."

Amidst the commotion, Ialasam Gelma weaved through the gathering crowd. His hat, almost completely covering his nose. His gun tucked safely inside his jacket. He paid no attention to the crowd surrounding the police vehicle. Ialasam overheard someone mentioning Susan's name. He sneaked passed one unnoticed, and glided along the path which Susan had previously taken.

Two blocks down the highway towards the river, Ialasam could hear the roadside commotion notched down and the sound of the river getting louder. Ialasam continued walking towards the cluster of bamboos leading towards the river.

Dua suddenly emerged from behind the bamboos without so much of a warning. Ialasam felt as if he had walked right into a clear glass wall without noticing it.

"Where is she?" Ialasam asked. Dua looked completely confounded. "Don't play dumb Dua," said Ialasam, coolly, "I'm talking about Susan. Where is she? "

"What do you want with her?"

"I'm the police officer, I ask questions, you answer, you do not get to ask the questions." Ialasam said. "Where is Susan?"

"She's beside the river."

"You left her alone?"

"Yeah."

Ialasam gave a sarcastic laugh. Dua stood there confused. "You are useless," said Ialasam. "You truly belong up in the mountain with your grandmother."

"Why are you saying this?"

"Dua, we all know about her rigorous sexual doggedness, and with your secret fantasies about her which your grandmother so movingly told me, it would have been enough stimulus for you to relieve yourself."

"Stop this."

"No sane man would have let an opportunity like that go by."

"How did –"

"Come on Dua," said Ialasam, "You think you are the first one she has tried to seduce?" Ialasam Gelma was tormenting Dua, and he was doing one hell of a job. Dua couldn't stand listening to Ialasam so he tried to walk away from him,

"I'm going home. I can't listen to you anymore."

"That's right Dua," said Ialasam, "Run home to your grandmother and tell her how close you came to being a man."

"What do you want from me!" Dua's words hung in the air. Ialasam Gelma looked strangely unhappy.

"You disappoint me," said Ialasam. "When the opportunity presents itself your pathetic moral principles still fight to remain a big part of your miserable existence. Thomas is a brute. You would have done us all a favour if you had taken Susan right there on the rocks."

"What is your problem?"

"I'm not the one with the problem Dua. You are the one with the problem." Ialasam said.

"Now, I am going to do something which you should have done tonight." Dua stood mystified as Ialasam walked away from him towards the river, supposedly to find Susan.

"Where are you going?" Dua called after. "What are you going to do?"

"I'm going to look for Susan. And when I do …..she is going to have me inside her."

"You can't be serious?"

Ialasam continued walking away without a response. After Ialasam had gone out of sight beyond a cluster of reeds Dua followed him.

Chapter 14

Dua followed Ialasam in a safe distance and stood out of sight and watched as Ialasam briskly glided over towards the cluster of bamboos beside the river. Dua's mind drifted off, further back to the first day he had set eyes on Susan.

It was a perfect sunny afternoon. She stood beside the highway in her shorts; laughing and giggling without the intention to provoke men. She was unaware of the effect she was having on motorists until a bus nearly ran astray.

Dua chuckled at the thought, now as he was watching he saw that Ialasam had arrived at the spot where Susan was sitting. Dua remained oblivious in the shadows and watched with racing curiosity.

Susan set with her legs folded on a patch of grass eyeing Ialasam as if demanding an explanation of some sort. Susan clearly had that ability to emanate the need for love before men.

Now seated, Susan kept eyeing Ialasam without a word. "You look lonely Susan." Said Ialasam. "Mind if I join you?"

"Why do the nice guys always show up late?"

"Beats me," said Ialasam.

He seemed to be fighting hard to maintain composer, fiddling in his trousers pocket, he produced a packet of cigarettes, and a lighter, he gave it to Susan before settling down next to her without coming into contact.

Susan desperately needed a smoke. Ialasam flicked the lighter and lit Susan's

"Thanks. Did anyone see you come here?" Susan asked.

"Nope. No one saw me."

"Good." Susan smiled. Both Susan and Ialasam set in silence and allowed the nicotine to take effect. Dua watched, he could see the way Susan was sitting had a touch of innocence and vulnerability, the mix would be perversely satisfying to any man Dua thought. Susan smoked and pretended not to notice Ialasam's eyes running all over her body, "It's impolite to stare at something that does not belong to you." Susan said, without looking at Ialasam.

"Sorry, I just couldn't help it. It's not every day I get to sit next to a beautiful women."

"I can see that." said Susan, not seeing at all. Ialasam kept his gaze.

"What do you mean?"

"I'm a married woman; I can't have other men looking at me like that. I feel violated." Susan said, giggling. She said it in a way like she wanted the opposite of what she was saying. She was enjoying it, loving the effect her body could have on the male libido. Ialasam didn't come to play games, he looked Susan square in the eyes.

"Are you happy where you are?" The smiles and giggles immediately disappeared from Susan's face. Susan didn't speak. "You are not married to Thomas. You are trapped in a relationship with him. I don't think you are happy where you are. I can see it in your eyes," said Ialasam. Susan felt a knot in her stomach.

"Is it that obvious?"

"Yes, it is."

"I made a mistake by marrying Thomas. I'm going to divorce him and go back to my people. I really hate him." Susan uttered bitterly. Ialasam could see that Susan was emotionally vulnerable,

"Susan, I am tired of seeing you like this. Each time Thomas gets away with it a piece of you is lost. This will go on until one day you will no longer have the will to love again."

"That is my greatest fear – what am I going to do?"

"Even the score with him."

"How? – How can someone like me stand up against the magnanimous man?"

"He's no man. He's a pathetic coward. The only thing keeping him afloat these days is his silver tongue, behind all his pretentious existence is a weak man who is afraid of his own shadow."

"Sounds like you know him well."

"I know enough" said Ialasam. "Tell me Susan, how much do you hate Thomas?"

"I really hate him."

"Well, that makes the two of us," said Ialasam. Susan walked right into that one. She didn't speak. Ialasam drew closer, narrowing the gap in between them, moving closer, closer, and the gap in between them ceased to exist. In one swoop Ialasam pulled Susan beside him and kissed her, Susan didn't fight it, she'd done enough fighting for one night, she simply hung, powerless, like a gazelle in a lion's jaws.

Dua gasped from his hiding place; he couldn't process what he was seeing. Susan was locked inside Ialasam's rock solid chest. She surrendered herself, sinking further into his embrace. Ialasam slid his hands like a snake all over her body, grabbing all her merchandise like a thief. Susan moaned with delight –

This man knows exactly what he's doing. Susan didn't realise her panties had somehow wondered off until Ialasam flipped her around rudely and entered from the back. Susan moaned yet again. The river applauded behind them.

Dua stood motionless and witnessed helplessly as Ialasam Gelma devoured Susan. Dua closed his eyes hoping it was all a bad dream. When he opened his eyes he caught Ialasam Gelma looking directly at him. Ialasam smiled derisively at Dua while he was hard at it, pounding rigorously till his face melted into a ugly grimace, and he let out a long, indulgent, delightful moan, filling Susan up.

Dua fainted.

Chapter 15

"Pipe down and stand back, ladies and gentlemen, please!" cried an elderly man. "Stand well back! The police are trying to do their job! Give them space to breath, most of you haven't had shower for a year it's disgusting in here! "

"Speak for yourself Jimmy!" A youth shouted amongst the crowd. Sassy giggles broke out inconspicuously amongst the youth's cronies scattered in the crowd. The elderly man fumed with rage, "Who said that!"

"Your son said it Jimmy!" Added someone. Jimmy withdrew, he couldn't think of a comeback.

The young women folks who gathered around were somewhat thrilled by the spectacle. Many of them quietly squealed with pleasure clutching on to the arms of their friends.

"Everyone listen!" Thomas shouted on top of his voice. "What happened already happened, the police are not here to listen to your grievances, save it for the court, they are here to prevent this fight from escalating. Let's be quiet and listen to what they have to say!"

A paunchy man with wide hips and very short legs steps in, "What is going to happen about the destruction of my store!" And to Thomas, he said. "I want the people who are responsible for this to compensate me!"

"You worry too much about money!" Thomas said. "Go home and sleep!"

"Damn you, Thomas! You caused this!"

"I didn't cause anything you bloody sorcerer!"

"I'm a sorcerer? You big nose bastard!"

"You take that back!"

"That's enough!" Nem ordered. "My men and I are not here to sort out your meaningless fight! We came here to give you a warning because in recent times this section of the Highway has been classified as a Red Zone!" Nem was now looking at a sea of dumbfounded locals. Nem had to explain. "Can anyone guess what I mean by the term Red Zone?" The people mumbled to each other without any response.

"What it basically means is," said Nem. "This stretch of the Highway from here to Talis has seen a rapid increase in crime in the past couple of weeks. Now, an executive problem by any order has come all the way from the very top for us to correct this as necessary!" The people remained quiet. "We have information that a group of men are responsible for all of these crimes" said Nem. "These men are all escapees from Boimo Prison in Lae. Some people here are harbouring these criminals!"

"Who is harbouring these criminals? Speak up now!" Cried an old man. "Find out who is harbouring these low lives' and raze their houses!"

"Yeah! We are not going to pay the price for them!" Cried another man. An uproar erupted. Curses and heated remarks were thrown at each other from all angles. Another fight seemed imminent. Nem drew out his revolver and fired a shot into the sky. The locals shrieked and quieted down.

"Protecting the highway is my priority!" Said Nem. "If you want to kill each other please go into the forest and do it, not by the roadside. This is a national Highway! My concern is the welfare of everyone in the Highlands who uses this road. This is not your road, register that in your thick skulls!"

Nem paused letting his remarks sink into the people's heads. Literally. His words came out with the authority of the crown that night. The people lowered their heads more out of respect than fear.

"I do not want to deal with your rubbish beer fights on my Highway while I'm trying to do my job!" Said Nem. "You are adults, take some responsibilities and help me out, let's work together on this. You are not the problem or my enemy, my problem are the men responsible for the highway holdups. They are enemies of the state, do you understand?" The people hummed. Another police car packed with officers also arrived.

"If any of you have information that will assist us in our investigation you can come and see me privately at the station." Nem said. "Also, take note that our come good Governor has placed a ten thousand kina reward for the capture of these criminals, our local MP for SSY has also pledged another ten thousand, so there is a total of twenty thousand kina for anyone who has information that will lead us to the capture of these criminals."

The people were all stirred up with solidarity. Nem could see that the inclusion of a monetary reward was the underlying factor.

"Starting tomorrow there will be a swift police operation." Said Nem. "We will come down hard on anyone who we suspect of harbouring these criminals! We don't want to do it but we have no choice. We have to find these men before they cause anymore harm to the public and our reputation, try to beat us to it if you are interested in that juicy reward." The people started talking to each other. Nem was no longer paying attention to them.

"Alright, toss the men who are involved in the fight at the back of that car!" Nem ordered. And to Kua he said. "You get in the car with me."

It was done; Kua's two friends including three locals who had allegedly attacked them were squashed up with three policemen in the other ten-seater. Kua and his two assailants were cramped up with the six policemen at the back of Nem's ride. Their skin rubbing against each other, Kua fought the urge not to make eye contact or snatch the gun from one of the officer's and shoot the two men. Kua hated the fact that he was sitting inside a cramped-up vehicle with the two men who had ruined his night.

Kua ground his teeth and clenched his fists. One of the officers noticed, "everyone cool it till we get to the station." The officer said, arrogantly. "We do not want to hear you speak or do anything stupid."

Commander Nem glared at them from the front seat. "Put a muzzle on your mouths." Said Nem. "Last thing I need is you knuckle heads reaching for my boys' guns and start shooting each other. I just washed this car, don't get blood or sweat on the floor or you will lick it off with your tongue."

Nem pulled his door shut and instructed the driver to go.

Chapter 16

Dua walked sombrely up the mountain with his hands behind his back and his head hung low. The image of Ialasam and Susan's aggressive love making under the moon lit sky beside the river erupted like fireworks inside his head every step of the way. One does not easily get over such an ordeal.

Dua tried rattling his head to rid the images, but he just couldn't. He couldn't grasp what Susan was thinking despite the dangers of being caught, in an open area, beside the river, while there were people at the roadside, with guns, trying to sort out the mess which would put her at the centre of it.

Seductive danger, Dua thought. Susan had Ialasam pursuing her so feverishly that he lost control and he was unaware of the dangers. A rational and repressed Dua considered the notion that danger and death strangely added emotional spice and seemed somewhat erotically appealing.

Dua wasn't bitter or the least jealous as he should be, but in a strange way he was somewhat content with the notion that someone else had the audacity which he himself lacked to relieve Susan from her misery. The thought alone was absurd but Dua couldn't think of anything else to supress this strange feeling inside.

Dua stopped somewhere and looked up to the night sky as if seeking divine guidance in these tormenting times, Lord give me strength. Dua kept moving again, he wanted to think about something else but he could not shake that image out of his head.

Dua felt a bit sorry for Thomas, Susan was surely not a housewife, she may be bought with a brides price, but she was still looking to be on the market. Her background had deprived her of something critical: affection. Her deepest need was to feel loved and desired, which made her seem constantly vulnerable, like a little girl craving protection.

She emanated this need for love before men. Dua finally arrived home and caught his grandmother sitting all alone waiting for him. When he approached her, she held out her hand and started sobbing,

"I am sorry Dua my boy, forgive me, for what I did tonight was evil," said Grandma. "I am ashamed of my actions. I foolishly put you in danger, and it was very selfish of me."

"Hay, you are not a bad person. You are an incredibly brave old woman, I'm proud of you." Dua said, consolingly.

"Proud of me?"

"Yes."

"What the hell are you proud of me for?"

"Grandma, not tonight please. I saw something down by the riverside that is troubling me. I really can't think straight tonight."

"What did you see?"

"I really shouldn't say it – "

"Oh C'mon, after what I just did tonight I'm pretty sure I can handle just about anything, try me Dua."

Dua was hesitant, he wasn't sure how to begin.

"Well, I followed Ialasam. I followed him down to Wara Simbu."

"And?"

"Well, I saw him, I saw him with Susan. I saw them by the riverside."

"Susan? You mean that girl you admire?"

"Not admire Grandma. I don't have feelings for her, I just – "

"Sure, whatever. What did she do with that monster Ialasam?"

"I saw them making love."

"Did you report that to her husband?"

"No, I did not. I didn't want her to get in trouble –"

"I'm sorry, what did you say?"

"Thomas might kill her. I don't want her blood on my hands." Grandma was fighting hard to maintain composer. Dua could tell she was struggling to supress her frustration. Grandma had this blind hatred for immoral women.

"So you didn't report, I see," said Grandma. "And what did you do?"

"I just saw them and left."

"You watched them didn't you? You watched the whole fiasco unfold. You know who else does that?"

"Who?"

"Perverts. That's who. Are you one?"

Dua sighed, he was too tired to argue. Dua eased back on the floor next to the fireplace, and rested his head, "Goodnight Grandma. Love you."

"Oh stop it please. I don't want love from a pervert grandson." Dua chuckled at the remark and closed his eyes hoping Grandma would find something useful to do and stop talking. Dua was too tired, and he dozed off much quicker than he expected.

Chapter 17

As dawn breaks at Wara Simbu the next day, a few broods of those that had dwelled on this land since the beginning of time were peacefully tucked in their beds, stuck on the other side, unaware of reality. The mornings are usually the coldest. The early birds ventured out of their houses with steaming coffee mugs in hand, some mugs big enough for two people to share. They were in their jackets, some in their blankets, standing in front of their houses with their coffee mugs and cigarettes, taking a piss discreetly...others less so.

One or two stiffly brave the misty ice-cold river to bath, sending chills up the spines of those that looked on in the warmth of their jackets and blankets.

The cry of Highway Mack's and PMV busses, travelling from Lae, and now struggling to climb the Prenoreqwa hill echoed all around Wara Simbu like an early morning bell. The teary looks on the drivers faces somewhat coordinated well with the exhausting sound emitted by the machine on which they rode in.

Two kilometres from Wara Simbu up the eastern stretch of the highway, a shirtless man broke out of the mist and scampered onto the highway with a terrified look on his face. He was wheezing for air as he tried to utter something while he was still on the run. He was struggling; his pants had slipped all the way down despite the belt he wore, exposing his bare butt chicks.

Three other men popped up behind him and screamed curses while on hot pursuit. They were advancing fast and furiously. The one being chased tried looking over his shoulder, unfortunately he tripped over his own footing, fell awkwardly and slid on the rough tar surface. The skin on his palm were scraped off.

He crawled gasping for air and felt he couldn't go on any further. He knelt down and looked at his wounded hands with incredulity; the white inside flesh gradually turned red with pods of blood instantly accumulating and dripping down like raindrops. On his knees, he surrendered.

His adversaries who had now arrived looked down on him from where they stood. Fuming with rage. They were all muscular men, with eyes as remote as the region from which they hailed.

"Get up Gigmai! Get on your feet!" They screamed in unison and erected him by the armpits. There was not a single trace of remorse in their eyes.

"I swear I have no idea!" Gigmai pleaded. "You have to believe me. This is a mistake!"

"Give us their names now!"

"I don't know anything I swear on my mother's grave."

"You lying sorcerer. Why are you covering up for these men?"

"Why would I be covering up for them? I don't even know them. I also want them captured bro. We are on the same side here guys!"

"Same side?"

"I swear to God I don't know anything…..I don't have the courage to pull off Highway robberies, this is bigger than me. I only steal women's underwear!" His assailants had to suppress their laughter at the final remark.

"We know that Gigmai," said one of them. "We are not asking if you are involved in the robberies. But we know you have been harbouring some men. Give us their names and spare yourself."

"I get visited by unknown people every day of the week. I sell homebrew. They are my customers! I only sell stuff to people….. most of them I don't even know."

"Gigmai, there is a twenty-thousand-kina bounty on these men. If you know something and you are hiding, we will beat it out of you. Just give us the names of the men that have visited you in the last four weeks."

"I have no idea what you people are talking about," Gigmai said defiantly. "You are searching for something which you cannot find because it doesn't exist."

"What do mean?"

This time Gigmai raised his head and answered almost in a whisper, "Has it ever occurred to you people, how and why after all these highway robberies you cannot identify at least one suspect?"

"Why is that?"

"Because they are ghosts. If they want to be known or seen they will allow it. And you people think these ghosts would have anything to do with someone like me? I am not even in their league."

"You speak like you know them. Let's see what the police make of that." Said the one standing on Gigmai's right.

Gigmai immediately turned to his right. "No no no please no police, you know what will happen if they get me, don't do this –"

"Shut up, there is going to be a police operation today, consider yourself as our sacrificial lamb."

"There has to be another way. I can't go to the police they are going to hang me for stealing those police boots….. wait wait wait, I have a small pig at my house, that's right. I will give it to you guys as compensation for your trouble, that's all I have just let me go."

The trio looked at each other. Gigmai was trying to bribe his way out of his predicament. "Alright, take us to the pig. Once we have it you can go." They agreed.

Four kilometres away, three RPNGC marked Toyota Land Cruiser Ten-Seater gunned down Prenoroqwa Hill. The Cruisers occupied both lanes of the highway, oncoming vehicles from the Eastern Highlands had nowhere else to go accept run into nearby bushes or simply make way. Pedestrians and vendors fled the roadside. Commander Kibre Nem rode in front of the convoy with his specially handpicked men. Yesterday Nem had issued a warning, today he was following up on progress.

"If these people do not give us something to work with," Nem said, "we will ransack the whole damn place. We will start from Numinma and move down. We will flush out these criminals from wherever they are. When you want something done right you have to do it yourself." Nem turned to face the driver. The daredevil driver nodded.

"Affirmative boss."

Chapter 18

T he memories materialised slowly.....like bubbles surfacing from the darkness of a bottomless well.

Dua stood beneath the crimson moon watching his hut consumed by fire. The smell of smoke hung everywhere. The mournful cries of human suffering echoing all around.

Dua could hear the cries inside his head. The tormenting cries grew louder. Dua held his head in awe , and he took a step forward and saw people still alive writhing in agony inside the furnace.

Dua transfixed his gaze and saw vividly a woman and two children burning alive. Gasping with horror Dua couldn't do anything but watch. The fire, like a terrifying monster kept devouring without mercy. He looked around frantically for help. On the far side someone materialised out of the dark and paced towards him.

"Please help me!" Dua shouted over, but his voice made no sound. The stranger kept walking towards Dua without a response. His face barely visible. "Please help me!" Dua again shouted. Dua froze when the stranger finally came into full view. The stranger was Ialasam Gelma.

There was not a glint of emotion registered on his face. Suddenly a hideous smile gradually swept across his face, "it's time you join them." Said Ialasam Gelma.

Before Dua had a second to comprehend Ialasam Gelma lurched himself at Dua, both men flung into hell.

Dua bolted awake, shouting! The room was dark. He was alone. The smoky odour inside his hut that had mingled with his dream filled the air, and somewhere outside birds twittered. He looked around, and vaguely worked out his surrounding despite the strong rays of sunlight passing through the gaps. Gradually, the fog in his eyes lifted and he saw he was sleeping beside the fireplace.

Still troubled by the dream, Dua sluggishly lifted himself up and headed for the door. He pulled the door open accompanied by the old man's groan; the sunlight charged inside sending him into blindness momentarily. He stepped outside dazed. The scorching sun beat down hard. The air was lively and attended by the familiar stench of rotten coffee husks.

Dua shook his head, he overslept, he couldn't believe he had woken up this late. He glanced across the vast mountainous scenery; the faint sound of a light aircraft progressively got smaller as it went further out, heading south east, over the colossal scrum of blue mountains. The vast blanket of infinite light blue sky stretched all the way to the ends of the earth.

On eye level Dua could see Kundiawa Town and its death-defying airstrip. Initially in the 1960's, Qantas would send their cadet pilots for a stint flying light aircraft in the Territory. Some of them never made it back to Australia. Flying by the seat of your pants was considered normal in a time where navigation aids were mostly absent.

Dua snapped out of his thoughts and headed around the hut in search of his grandmother. There was no sign of his grandmother there. He called around, shouted in every direction, and waited for a response. Nothing.

Mona wasn't inside the shed either. Dua stood around and felt a strange void. Suddenly the dream materialised in his head, in his mind's eyes he saw his grandmother screaming in agony inside the furnace, chills ran down his spine. Dua ran down the mountain.

He knew that the only place his grandmother would be was beside her riverside garden.

Dua halted momentarily to spot any sign of life at the foot of the mountain, but there was none. Nonetheless Dua continued his descent. In less than five minutes, Dua was already at the foot of the mountain.

He immediately went in search for his grandmother. There was no sign of Grandma or Mona anywhere. Dua stopped walking and scanned the riverside. The breeze gently caressed his cheeks, and where it went the reeds flowers, spikelet's with tufts of silky hair swayed back and forth, nodding in approval. All along the river bank reeds grew in vast unbroken stands forming dense, impenetrable 'fence-like' masses.

The place looked innocent, yet the unusual quietness of the day had a rather eerie touch to the atmosphere. Dua gazed across the river; Waghi ran fast yet graceful.

The gentle sound of the surroundings had a drowsy effect. Dua felt as if he was receding into a trance-like state. In that moment he saw it…. on the far bank, a man stood facing him, motionless, solemn, his face hidden by a shroud.

The man slowly revealed his face and seemed to be looking directly at Dua. Dua couldn't work out his face. The man moved toward him, holding out his hands, as if beckoning for help. "Dua" the man whispered, "Run".

The words were spoken inside his head. Dua shook his head violently and snapped out of it. He looked back across the river and the man was no longer there. Dua jolted up at the familiar loud-mouthed laughter of his grandmother coming from across, near the river banks behind the reeds. Who could she be talking to this time? Dua thought.

Dua curved around the reeds and saw his grandmother sitting on the dirt smiling and paying close attention to someone who stood hidden behind the cluster of reeds on that side. Dua paused where he stood and called over, "Grandma who are you talking to?"

Startled, Grandma turned around and saw Dua standing there. A short stubby man materialised from behind the reeds and smiled. "Good day to you Dua."

"Robin? What are you doing here?" Dua thought out loud.

Robin smiled. "It's a free world Dua". Dua realised the discourtesy of the question and immediately regretted it.

"I'm sorry my head is all over the place this morning". Dua apologised.

"It's alright. I sometimes forget things too. I woke up one morning saw my wife and screamed thinking a stranger had broken into my room."

"Really?"

"True story." Robin paused for a second. "She actually was a stranger, that was the first time I brought her home drunk after a party. And she never left. Seven years of head ache".

"You mean seven years of bad luck," Robin laughed at his own remarks. Dua couldn't understand what Robin was going through. He had no idea.

"So technically you were not married at that time." Dua asked.

"What do you mean?"

"I mean the first time you brought her home drunk?"

"What difference does it make? I shouldn't have brought her home, now look at me. I'm stuck here. I could have been a businessman you know."

"Well look on the bright side, at least you have a wife and children to go home to."

"Yeah, I guess you are right about that. Two hungry children to be exact."

"I would say you are a decent man Robin."

"Thank you, Dua. Why don't you come by and see me this Saturday, it's not healthy living alone".

"Yeah, I think that is a great idea."

"Good. I'm sure my wife would love to have you as our guest."

"I'm sure she would," said Dua. "I have heard some pretty exciting things about her and I intend to find out for myself."

Robin thought Dua's remark didn't come out right, Robin had to say something, "You mean you have heard she's a great cook," Robin said, smiling. "And you intend to find out."

"Oh cooking too, amongst others."

"Such as?"

"She loves having young men around her. It makes her so happy."

Robin was suddenly uncomfortable with Dua's sudden shift in demeanour, "Look, let's not get ahead of ourselves here," Robin said. "I am trying to have a decent conversation, Dua."

"A decent conversation about your indecent wife."

"Pardon me?"

Dua's voice morphed into a deeper, mellifluous whisper, "Your wife, I hear her legs open like a charity organisation." The smile had disappeared from Dua's face. It was as if a different person was standing there. Robin felt a chill race through his body,

"Dua, what are you saying? What the hell is going on?"

"You heard me Robin. Let's not pretend putting up a show with fake laughter and smile like I give a damn about your useless personal life." Dua said, taunting. "You are such a sad person, you need to get out of here before something really bad happens. I will give you to the count of three to disappear from this place and never come around here again. One – two –"

Robin clutched his fishing rod tightly and recoiled, his world began to spin as he realised he was dealing with a mad man. He fled from Dua without turning back.

Chapter 19

Ialasam Gelma waded down the Chimbu River from an inconspicuous spot; the river there flows gracefully into Waghi River. Sheltered in the foliage. He wanted to take the shortcut to Dogor.

Ialasam got to the other side of the river and ventured up the steep slope that was riddled with reeds and thorns. After less than five minutes of fighting through the bushes he arrived at Dogor; a small hub. Ialasam braved the inquisitive stares by residents and a few hostile canines as he paced on the unsealed limestone pathway, heading towards the roadside.

At the roadside there was a small marketplace with vendors, and customers wondering aimlessly. A lonesome trade store, and a crowded liquor shop stood further down with a sign that reads: SAVE WATER, DRINK BEER.

Ialasam wasn't amused, nor was he interested in the informal economic activities that were going on. He was there for a different purpose.

What Ialasam came for arrived. Further down from the crowded liquor shop, at a small intersection, a white double cab Toyota Hilux materialised slowly. Ialasam walked down towards the parked Hilux. When he arrived, the lone driver motioned him to the front seat. Ialasam got in.

Comfortably seated in the front seat, Ialasam could see that the driver's hands were shaking on the steering wheel. He was a tall skinny man in his early thirties, his eyes were those of a man struggling with marijuana and porn addiction, the latter seemed to have taken a toll on his life. The driver was in his work uniform; light yellow with stripes of purple here and there, the breast pocket read: KUNDIAWA BANK.

"What's going on John?" Asked Ialasam. "I don't know if I can do this." "Hey hey, we talked about this, just calm down and relax." Ialasam whispered.

John turned to face Ialasam, not sure if Ialasam heard him right. Ialasam could see that John was on the verge of a major nervous breakdown.

"Take a deep breath. Tell me everything you think that I should know." Ialasam said.

"Listen, I'm not sure if I want to be a part of this anymore." John said, edgily. "You are not part of anything, I can assure you." Said Ialasam.

"Listen. The person I am talking with doesn't even know you, no one knows you, the information comes from you, goes to me, I give it to my contact and he gives it to some other people whom I've never met. As far as this channel is concerned you are in the safest possible zone. Trust me. I am the one putting out my neck here, and believe me this guy's not the type of people I want to let down."

John considered Ialasam thoughtfully for a while as if trying to figure out how this guy got recruited into the Police College. "Alright." Said John. "If they are going to do this….. it has to be done tomorrow."

"What?"

"Tomorrow. If they come a day later than tomorrow, they will miss out on the biggest pay-out of their lives."

"What's going to happen a day after tomorrow?"

"The volt will be empty." John said. "Tomorrow afternoon a plane arrives to redistribute the surplus cash that had overlapped from last year. All unfit bills will also be transferred back to Pom for formal record and shredding. What will remain are marked bills. I don't expect that to make any difference but what's the point of having money you can't spend?"

Ialasam stared at John. John looks back and saw in his eyes something odd. He couldn't place it. John was uncomfortable now. "I have to get back," John said.

"You just got here. You still haven't told me anything yet."

"I'm going to break it to you right now," said John. "Despite the increased use of credit transections, the Papua New Guinea economy still uses a massive amount in cash every day."

"What does that got to do with the bank?"

"Everything bro. The Bank of Papua New Guinea keeps surplus notes in cash depots around the country. You see. the money moves in predictable waves. The Christmas period is when the most money is in circulation, but February is the quietest time of the year, when surplus cash is stored at a few cash centres, including Kundiawa Bank."

"I see. With spending peaking at weekends, cash tends to flow back to depots in the middle of the week." Ialasam added.

"Exactly. Mid-February represents a crest of the cash wave. If you hit the bank tomorrow as I have said you will strike gold."

"How much are we talking about here?"

"Three point five million."

"Shit." Ialasam now understood why John was scared. Both men sat in silence allowing the enormity of the discussion to settle.

"Look, I have to go," said John. "I'm going to call in sick tomorrow, I hate to be around when shit blows out of proportion – "

"Don't, If you do that it's going to be suspicious. Just go to work, be on guard, keep your head down and act normal." Said Ialasam.

"It's easy for you to say. This is almost like telling my enemies how they are going kill me."

"Listen. After all this you will get your share. I will make sure of it."

"I appreciate that. Now get out of my car, I have to go."

Ialasam hopped out as quickly as he got in, and shut the door. He stood outside and gave an assuring nod. As John was starting to drive out Ialasam removed a parcel from his back pocket and approached. He offered the parcel to John, "here is what you asked for."

John received the gift. "Thanks, I really needed this." John tore the plastic wrapping immediately to examine the content. Inside the wrapping what appeared like cow dung, sticky hicky, mushed together. John beamed. "This is gold," said John.

"Green gold. This is the last of it. Only the best for you."

"I appreciate it." John said, smiling for the first time.

Ialasam was less interested in John's approval. All that interested him was the information John had given him. Ialasam lifted his phone right after the car had left and made a call. His face motionless as he waited for the call to be answered.

Chapter 20

Gigmai led the trio down a dirt track that led to an old abandoned coffee garden. They had walked some distance from the highway. The trio made sure they were close to Gigmai at all time in case Gigmai tried to make a run for it. But, Gigmai wasn't in any hurry, he tried stirring up casual talk but the trio seem only interested in getting to the pig.

Their ordeal beside the road seemed forgotten. Gigmai had a way of bouncing back. Anyone passing by would simply think they were four best friends taking a morning stroll, "This place used to be a beautiful garden," Gigmai was saying. "The magistrate and his wife made a fortune from this garden."

"So I've heard." Said the one behind Gigmai, sounding less interested.

"The dry season has ruined everything." Gigmai said, making a show of sounding concerned. The trio didn't respond. For once Gigmai was right. All around thorns and shrubs consumed what was left of the garden. The dried earth's crust cracked everywhere beneath the feet of the dried-up coffee trees. Not a single green leaf could be seen on the coffee trees. The surrounding could have been a scene right out of the Kalahari Desert.

Gigmai went on, he kept talking about the dry season and how he was struggling to survive. The trio heard only empty prattling. They kept walking further down. Gigmai finally stopped walking, "Anyways, I told the magistrate that if the dry season continues for another month we could all die you know." Gigmai said. "We need to move –"

"Gigmai enough. If you continue talking for another minute you could die you know. Now where is that pig?" The one behind Gigmai cut in impatiently.

"Relax, we are here already." Gigmai said. Pointing to a long pig shed beneath the bamboos. The trio turned to look.

"Gigmai this is the magistrate's pig shed."

"I know. I asked the magistrate to keep my small pig in with the rest of his. I couldn't afford to look after the pig you know. His wife must be here somewhere let's go check," said Gigmai.

Gigmai waltzed up confidently to the gardening hut and called around for the magistrate's wife. The trio remained standing and watched. They were sceptical. But they realised Gigmai had no reason to lie, his life was hanging in the balance here. They remained standing and noticed Gigmai talking with someone who was sitting down, well hidden behind the bamboos.

The trio looked at each other and walked over. When the trio arrived behind Gigmai, they saw an old woman sitting down on the dirt. It was the magistrate's mother. She was ancient; all skin and bone, much like the coffee trees they saw on their way here. Her eyes were all misty, her wrists were riddled with black wristbands, she was missing four fingers which she had cut off many years ago, each finger representing the death of someone very dear to her, a self-inflicted punishment largely practiced in the highlands region as sign of deep sorrow in the passing of a loved one.

"Mina, when is she coming back?" Gigmai was asking her. "I really need to see her right now." The old woman kept looking at Gigmai and smiled helplessly. She had only one canine tooth remaining.

Gigmai heaved a sigh, "the magistrate's wife must have gone up to the road," said Gigmai. "The road is probably full of cops already so I can't possibly be seen around there as we agreed on. So one of you have to go up there and summon her." The trio looked at each other.

"The road is too far, who wants to walk up that distance?"

"I'm just saying. We can wait for her, I have no problem with that. But she might take forever to get here." Said Gigmai. The trio considered Gigmai carefully. There was not a trace of scepticism on his disfigured face and bloodshot eyes.

"Well, can you just give us the pig now and inform her later?"

"Yeah, sure." Gigmai replied.

Gigmai walked past the old women to the pig shed. Gigmai held the rail and scanned the shed. There were seven pigs all separated in each cubicle. Four of the pigs were fully matured. Gigmai walked past the larger ones and finally stopped at the far end cubicle. "It's this one. Come help me bring her out!" Gigmai called over to the trio.

The trio walked over and inspected the animal. "It's much bigger than I thought." One of them said. "It's all yours now, I was going to sell it and use the money to travel to Lae but, anyways, go on, get it, and be gone." Gigmai said, with a flash of emotion.

The trio fervently removed the wooden fencing piece by piece from the marked cubicle until the shed was opened. Gigmai took the rope that was hanging from the shed's roof and handed it to them. They tied the rope around the pig's front right hoof and led the pig out. The pig complied without a struggle. They looked over and saw the old woman still smiling.

"I guess that settles it then. I'm going to leave you to it." Gigmai announced.

"Not so fast Gigmai. If you cross us we will skin you alive."

"Hey, I'm only doing this to stay out of prison, why would I make matters worse for myself? Consider this pig as my payment for immunity."

Chapter 21

The daredevil driver had guided the Cruiser to Numinma. Commander Nem instructed the driver to ease towards a crowd of men, women and children who were fervently standing beside the road and watching the convoy pulling in. Nem again instructed the driver to park in the midst of the crowd, as he so often does just for convenience's sake.

Seated comfortably in his seat, Nem looked down and saw six shirtless men, on the dirt, battered, and on their knees. "What's going on?" Nem questioned everyone who stood there. Everyone appeared almost panicky. Nem loved that effect he had on people,

"I want to hear the story from one person! The rest of you can concur." Nem said.

Everyone turned to face the local village magistrate. Nem was about to step out of the car when his mobile phone rang. He checked the caller ID and inhaled deeply. Then he closed the door and settled back in to take the call.

At Kundiawa Police Station, the Provincial Police Commander Kombri Gigma was moving through the corridors of the building with his cell phone pressed to his ear. He patiently waited as the call rang. Finally, Nem answered. "Yes?"

"Stop what you are about to do and stand down," PPC Gigma said. There was a long pause.

"What's going on?"

"The short guy that stood up to you last night is the Governor's cousin brother, and his son's a big shot human rights lawyer. Without an actual State of Emergency, we cannot carry out any raids. We can't afford it so abort mission and call off your men," Gigma said.

"Alright."

Gigma took a deep breath. "Return to HQ."

Nem ended the call, picked up the radio and informed his men that the mission was called off. He knew his men would be disappointed but there was nothing he could have done, the orders came from people who were above his pay grade, he was only there to comply, the repercussions for disobedience would have caused him and his team to lay dormant for a very long time, he wasn't going to risk it.

Nem sat for a moment to think of something he could do that will be in accordance with the law and at the same time produce results. Nothing. Lurking outside the car's open window the local magistrate and everyone else stuck their heads around eagerly to hear something from Nem.

Nem heaved a sigh as he opened the door to step out and address the people. He tucked his pistol as he stepped out, that was his signature move, he always wore a visible sidearm as a warning to anyone foolish enough to question the extent of his authority.

The local magistrate walked forward and gave Nem a firm handshake with a smile, "top morning to you Nem." Said the magistrate. "You were busy on the phone earlier, I was trying to tell you that we understood from the people at Wara Simbu that there was going to be raid today?"

"That's what we came here to do. But you can prevent that by giving us something to work with." Nem said, concealing the fact that the raid had just been called off. It was a calculated move.

"I understand. Trust me when I say this, that I want these criminals arrested or killed as much as you. What we have here are six men whom we believe are either working with the thugs or know something." Said the magistrate pointing to the six shirtless men huddled together on the dirt. "How you deal with them is the least of all our concern."

"How certain are you that these men might help this case?" Nem asked.

"I am very certain," said the Magistrate. "They are all known criminals around here, if there was anything out of the ordinary, they would be the first to know."

"So you didn't ask them if they knew something about the highway robberies?"

"Well, w-we did, but they just wouldn't open up. It's as if they are afraid to talk."

"They are afraid of what the actual highway robbers might do to them?"

"It seems that way."

"Is that so? Now what kind of people would terrify them so much that they would be willing to risk their lives to protect them?"

"I don't know."

"Bring one of them here and I'll show you." Nem instructed.

The local magistrate summoned the local men to bring one of the captives to Nem. They asked which one and Nem's trained eye specifically choose the one that trembled most. People who fear have something to hide. When the scaredy cat was brought in front of Nem, Nem regarded him carefully while puffing his monster brus. The scaredy cat was bony; his eyes were bulging out of his skull. Nem didn't speak. He raised the scaredy cat's chin up with his pistol.

"What's your name?" Nem asked.

The sacredy cat summoned his courage and said "Baundo."

"Listen Baundo," Nem said, "I am going to give you one golden opportunity in a lifetime to save yourself. Tell me something now, and I promise nothing will ever happen to you. You have my word."

Baundoy the scared cat trembled to a point where it was obvious to everyone around, he was shaking. Nem considered this and suppressed the rising anger inside. Nem personally made no bones about cowards. Nem had more respect for a thug who braves a gun fight then the one that flees the scene.

"I-I think the right person you should ask is Gigmai," said Baundo. "I heard there were strange men that have come to visit him. They say these men are really bad men from the East, since the day they have arrived the highway robberies in Talis started."

"It's true!" One of the captives concurred. "Gigmai is harbouring them!" The rest of the captives agreed in unison. "Gigmai knows who they are!"

"Are you referring to Gigmai the thief?" Nem asked.

"Yes, the very same." They all said.

"They same guy that stole all your shoes!" Stole my shoes? Nem quickly exchanged a gaze with one of the young police men. They both knew Gigmai very well. "So where is Gigmai then?" Nem asked, looking at the magistrate. "Shouldn't Gigmai be the one here?"

"Well he was chased by some of the guys here, he couldn't have gone far, I'm sure if they –" The magistrate immediately stopped talking when the corner of his right eye caught a small commotion some distance down the road. A woman was arguing with three young men. Nem also followed the magistrate's eyes. The situation down the road intensified, the woman was yelling curses at the young men. Nem turned to the magistrate,

"Isn't that your wife?" Nem asked. The magistrate left Nem hanging and walked over to see what was happening between his wife and the young men.

Nem signalled two police men to follow the magistrate.

When the magistrate neared the commotion, his wife was saying, "Yalkane! You men walk up here real smart with the pig as if you haven't done anything wrong! How much marijuana did you smoke with Gigmai before you came up here?"

"We told you we had no idea it was your pig! Gigmai lied to us!" The trio defended themselves.

"How stupid can you be? Do you think that low life, good for nothing, worthless human being has ever looked after a pig in his life? Gigmai set you up!"

"We didn't know! We swear to God! Here you can have the pig back." Said one of them, handing her the leash. "Your husband's mother didn't say anything so we thought Gigmai was telling us the truth."

The magistrate's wife snatched the leash, "Mina lost her hearing and sight a year ago you simpletons! Nowadays she just smiles at people! That sneaky sonofabitch knows about that!"

"Where is Gigmai?" The magistrate asked. The trio looked down and collectively let their minds roam all over Chimbu for an explanation but nothing surfaced. They were tongue tied under the hard scrutiny of the police men present. They couldn't possibly say they let Gigmai go. How could they?

One of the police officers moved forward, "Are you idiots deaf! The magistrate asked you a question! Where is Gigmai?" The trio didn't speak.

"Let's see what Nem says about that." The Magistrate said.

The two Police Officers motioned the trio to follow them to Nem's parked convoy. A small noisy crowd followed them. When the trio stood in front of Nem, they all had their heads down. Nem moved forward, "Where is Gigmai?" Nem asked.

The trio shook their heads, "He's gone."

"How so?"

"He tricked us and left." The magistrate's wife who was still frustrated tried to interject but the magistrate who saw this quickly put his hand on her mouth literally shutting her off.

"He tricked you and left?" Nem did a double take. The trio nodded,

"Yes."

"Hey! Raise your heads when I'm talking to you! What the hell happened?!" Nem roared. The trio shivered. They went pale suddenly. Nem couldn't bottle his fury any longer, he launched a mighty right hand that smashed on the skull of the one that stood in the middle, the punch had enough power to carry him a good four metres from where he stood, his lights went out before his body slammed on the dirt. He was out, cold. The other two immediately got on their knees,

"We had him boss! But then he bribed us with the pig and we let him go! We can get him back! Please, you have to understand if pigs weren't in short supply Gigmai would be here! It's dry season our stomach did the judgement, we had no control! We are sorry!"

Nem fought the temptation to kick one of them in the face but somehow managed to contain his anger, "I'm gonna pretend I didn't just hear what you said." Nem said. "Both of you are going to go and comb every piece of grass in this land until you find Gigmai. Your unconscious friend over there will remain in my custody until you bring me Gigmai. If you don't bring me Gigmai, your friend will be charged for aiding and abiding a convicted criminal and appear before the court. And then I'm gonna come back for you. Am I understood?"

Both men looked at each other before looking at Nem and nodded in unison. "Am I understood?" Nem asked again. "Yes boss." They answered.

"Now get the hell out of my sight before I change my mind." Nem said, and to the police men in sight he turned and said, "Toss their unconscious friend in the back of my car."

The two men immediately got on their feet and snaked past the crowd and disappeared.

Chapter 22

High upon the western Mountaintop that towered over Talis and that section of the Okuk Highway, five rugged looking men stood side by side; looking down.

At the foot of the mountain there was a huge commotion; men, women and children were shouting and arguing. There were three police vehicles parked beside the road.

Yesterday, the five men had rattled the bee hive and fled to their hideout at the banks of Waghi River, today they returned to see the hell they have raised burning out of control. Like watching agitated bees from a safe distance after disturbing the bee hive.

"Look at them down there, they don't know what hit them." Oscar broke the silence with a deep commanding voice. It was the same voice beside Waghi River the previous night, the ghost that almost gave Dua a heart attack. A ghost indeed.

Though he goes by the name Oscar, only a few people knew this. A lifetime of crime had earned him the name 'Ghost,' a name well suited for his disappearing acts.

Oscar turned to face his crew. He had a sharp spear-like nose that coordinated well with his beard. "That's the thing about men like us," said Oscar. "When they finally get us, we won't stand a chance."

The one named Kembol, who stood beside him nodded. "Poor guys down there….. all innocent men. This can only mean one thing."

"What?" Oscar asked.

"The police are getting desperate for results. They will comb every grassland in this area just to find us. Whatever you are planning Oscar it better be big and quick." Kembol said with a raspy Western Highlands accent.

"My contact has already found us a job," said Oscar. "But the risks are too great, but the reward's even greater. It has never been done before because no one is crazy enough to do it. That's why we are going to do it."

"What kind of job are we talking about here Oscar?" Asked Kembol.

"We are going to rob the Kundiawa Bank." Oscar said, with finality. Oscar looked around and saw no one disagreed. On his left side the inseparable Rento brothers from Eastern Highlands stood inches away from each other, followed by the shortest member of the gang Al Simon. Oscar knew they will not try to talk him out of it, only he himself has the power to call it off, which was why he took great deliberation before announcing it, either way these men would follow him directly to hell if they have to.

"How reliable is your source? Can we trust him?" Kembol asked.

"You don't have to trust my source. You only need to trust me. My contact is not stupid. He has seen my face. Be mindful of the consequences if you make a deal with the devil." Said Oscar.

"Your contact, where is he from?"

"He's a local. Lives around here. You will meet him today."

"Good. I'd like to see his face. Hey, remember the bank security guard in Lae?" Kembol asked.

"Yeah. What about him?" Said Oscar. "He thought we were going to come back and finish him off. He left his wife and ran away for good. No one has seen him since." Kembol said, smiling.

Oscar looked at Kembol and laughed. The rest of the gang followed suit. In a matter of seconds, a chorus of hideous laughter erupted on the mountain top as they broke out.

At the foot of the mountain, amidst the commotion, Commander Kibre Nem raised his head to the west and caught the final glimpse of five men disintegrating like mist at the summit. Nem looked down and felt the hunch in his gut. He suddenly realised he was looking at the wrong place the whole time.

Chapter 23

Sheltered in the foliage on the North Western gulch of Numinma, the clear crystal river called Membi Nilge, no less than a metre on average in depth, rolls quietly, like liquid glass, gliding down and curving it's way around the dark slate shale, revealing the pebbles, earth and sand beneath.

Membi Nilge is secluded from the raucous Wara Simbu, and provides a serene spot for those who prefer privacy. It's beauty often lures ignorant strangers into a swarm of degenerate youths indistinctly communicating with blood shot eyes, muscular shirtless men, and sweaty, nasty looking faces distilling illegal home brew, and rolling up blunts.

The milieu proves to be an ideal spot for illegal activities. The likes of Gigmai find sanctuary in Membi Nilge. Society rejects those who congregate in silence and brew trouble.

As in this and every other day, a group of men were busy pouring the sappy cocktail of weeks long fermented pineapple, banana, yeast, sugar mixed with water into an empty gas cylinder.

The cylinder's knob had been removed, and the sappy cocktail distinguished throughout the region as "white soup" is carefully and generously poured inside the gas cylinder. The men then inserted a funnel into the opening where the knob had been removed, the funnel had to withstand boiling temperature of 100 degrees, so they used copper funnels; it has to be inserted firmly to prevent any air from escaping around the joint.

Then they paste clay around the joint to prevent any steam from escaping. The air tight gas cylinder with all its content is placed over the furnace. The copper funnel runs through the water, and on the receiving end of the funnel the men desperately wait for the distilled "white soup" to pour into their containers.

Gigmai had escaped from his ordeal and joined his cronies. He was safe for now, but his mind was absent from the group. Little did the men know that Gigmai had just come from a dangerous predicament.

Gigmai knew very well he was still in trouble, he had created a greater problem just to escape from the immediate threat, the full weight of his mischievous deed will probably cost him a leg or an arm. But Gigmai also knows that no one apart from the police will dare touch him here.

As Gigmai sat there thinking, he saw Ialasam Gelma materialised behind the bushes downstream. Gigmai immediately got on his feet and had a quick glance at the men who were extracting the first distilled "white soup" called "kambe" at the receiving end of the copper funnel.

"The first one is the real nectar, what comes after is for your girlfriends. Keep that in mind." Gigmai said to the men and walked down stream to meet Ialasam in private.

The men understood what Gigmai meant. Five to six litters of "white soup" should produce at least a litre of raw "kambe". The first distillation is guaranteed to be potent, commercially ready, and should be separated from whatever that comes after.

Ialasam stood a distance downstream and saw Gigmai walking towards him, he could easily tell that Gigmai was in some sort of trouble by the way he was approaching. Ialasam could only imagine. Of course, Gigmai had the knack for trouble, wherever Gigmai went trouble was bound to follow, but now was certainly not the time to deal with his shit.

"They are on to me," Gigmai said before he came near. "I just had run in with three guys before I came here."

"Keep your voice down." Said Ialasam.

Gigmai came closer and sat on a rock. "They wanted me to talk," Gigmai said. "But I didn't tell them anything."

"Are you sure?" Ialasam asked.

"Am I sure of what?"

"Are you sure you didn't tell them anything? Because under threatening situations you might spill the bins without realising it."

Gigmai shot a questioning look. "What are you trying to say?"

"It doesn't matter. The good thing is you didn't say anything. A lot of very dangerous men are counting on us to keep our mouths shut." Ialasam said, quickly changing the subject.

"I didn't say a damn thing. Did you meet up with my guy from the bank?"

"Yes I did. He was very helpful."

"Good. And did you give him the drugs I sent?"

"Yeah, I gave it him."

"Alright. Listen, I can't stay here any longer. When are we going to Lae?"

Ialasam heaved a deep sigh trying to subdue his annoyance. "Your days of selling kambe will be over shortly. I just need one last job from you."

Gigmai considered Ialasam thoughtfully.

"Anything for you boss."

Ialasam looked at Gigmai in all seriousness. "I need you to go to Chuave right now. There is a guy in Migin by the name of Masane. You find him and tell him I sent you. He will know what to do."

"Masane? How do I find him?"

"Just ask the locals. Can you do that?"

"Yes boss."

"Good. Everything goes down tonight." Ialasam said with finality and walked away.

Chapter 24

Susan crossed the road over to the small roadside market nestled beneath bamboos and trees. A dozen heads could be seen afar beneath the shade as she approached.

She began to hear voices, indistinct at first but as she drew closer, she could make out familiar faces absorbed in playing cards. Susan couldn't help but think of an incident which occurred a while back.

At that time, people were crouching low as they are doing now, engrossed in their cards, while onlookers and critics stood around aimlessly but equally absorbed. They were all unaware of the approaching armed police men who were on foot patrol to cut out roadside gambling. The officers snuck in quietly and stood around and watched for almost a minute.

When the gamblers suddenly realised, they were surrounded, it was already too late to scramble. The police men rounded up the gamblers, shared the cards amongst them, and told them to start 'eating' the cards and swallow it. They did. Susan was unfortunately one of the gamblers at that time.

It was a very unpleasant experience for her. She had never gambled since. Susan shook her head to rid the humiliating memory as she arrived in front of at least four roadside vendors.

The first one was a happy looking old woman selling boiled corn, God knows how she managed to grow corn in this weather, Susan thought. Right next to the happy old woman to the right was another old woman looking bored as hell selling dried and shrivelled up greens. Next to boring old lady was another woman, probably in her mid thirties selling boiled eggs, she looked relaxed, boiled eggs sell quickly, she had nothing to worry about. On boiled egg's right was a young man in his late twenties selling Mareta; Susan couldn't tell whether he was skittish or jumpy, he probably stole those Mareta, Susan thought.

One of the gamblers broke a hacking cough and the Mareta guy immediately swung around. Yep, he stole those Mareta. Susan flipped a twenty kina on boiled eggs lady plastic mat, "I'm getting six of those." The vendor smiled nicely, "Thank you."

Susan bent down and picked the eggs and placed them inside her Bilum. She then stood up and waited for her change. She could feel the gazes of the other vendors on her, the Mareta guy ever so often kept glancing Susan's way.

I'm not buying stolen Mareta thank you, Susan thought.

"Can you hurry up with the change?" Susan said, impatiently. "I have to be somewhere."

"She needs to be back at the office, make it quick." The Mareta guy said, suddenly. "We don't want to keep her waiting." The sarcasm in his tone couldn't be missed. The other vendors giggled. The egg lady couldn't help it either.

Susan was startled, "I beg your pardon?"

The Mareta guy wasn't smiling. "You heard me." Something in his voice told Susan that he was looking for trouble.

"You know," Susan said, sighing. "I was really going to buy one of those Mareta. But you just blew it away. Good luck selling them."

"I'm not selling these Mareta," the young man said, seriously. "I just bought those from Mingande. I don't sell. I buy."

Susan looked slightly embarrassed, "Oh...well good for you." She said. "Good luck eating them."

Susan snatched her change from the egg lady. She needed to go home quickly, Mareta guy was clearly looking for trouble. "Don't get smart with me," the young man said again. "My cousin brother suffered a broken rib because of the shit you and your husband created here last night. If I were you I would choose my words carefully."

"I had nothing to do with that. You should tell that to Thomas."

"I don't need to talk to your stupid drunk husband." The young man said, fearlessly. "Me and my brothers are personally holding him responsible. If he doesn't sort out my cousin brother there is going to be trouble. I have nine brothers. Thomas is only one man. Tell your drunk husband to keep that in mind."

Susan looked around and saw that it was obvious everyone including the gamblers seem to be paying attention without showing it. No one dared speak. Apparently, a lot had happened last night while Susan was busy playing Russian Roulette with Ialasam Gelma down by the riverside.

Susan held her bilum tightly without saying another word and withdrew.

Chapter 25

Susan walked back furious from her roadside ordeal, but she had other pressing things in mind. She needed to talk to someone. She saw Thomas's smaller sister Martha sitting alone underneath the Wara Simbu bridge busy making a Bilum.

Susan walked over. Martha remained quiet; with the red scarf over her head, her bony face glimmered. She looked much younger than someone in her late-thirties, she was evidently skinny under the dark oversized mary blouse.

"Martha?" Susan said. "I need your help." Martha turned her head and faced Susan. Susan found it difficult to maintain her stance under Martha's regard. "Martha, you remember the last time I told you that Thomas had been talking silly in his sleep," said Susan. "Well, I haven't been completely honest with you, Thomas had been mentioning someone's name in his sleep, I think Thomas wants that person dead. This morning, I overheard him mentioning that same name over and over until he completely lost it."

Martha looked serious. "Whose name was he calling?"

"Dua. Thomas was calling Dua's name in his sleep. Kill Dua, Kill Dua, Kill him, Thomas was saying, Martha I'm scared, what is going on?"

Martha looked away from Susan, she seemed troubled by what Susan had said but yet she was distant, it was as if she didn't care.

"Martha, I need you to talk to me and help me understand things, I can't go on living like this, tell me something I don't know about Thomas please." There was silence again from Martha. She returned back to making her Bilum, while Susan fought the urge to slap her across the face but snapped out of it. Susan could see it was hopeless. Susan sighed heavily and tried to leave.

"You remind me of her," Martha said, suddenly. "So young and full of questions."

Susan settled down again. "Who are you talking about Martha?" Susan asked.

"Thomas's first wife. She was about your age, she was a very beautiful woman, I can still remember her smile."

"What happened to her?"

"She died. Killed herself. I was there that day. She hanged herself from this very spot above your head." Susan immediately looked up. She noticed that the bridge ran approximately ten to fifteen metres above ground level from where they were sitting, anyone hanged from that height wouldn't stand a chance.

"Why did she kill herself?" Susan asked.

"She couldn't find a way out of the predicament she was in," said Martha. "She had no other choice but to end her own life."

"What was her predicament? Martha please tell me what happened?" Susan suddenly felt a chill up her spine. The look on Martha's face and the manner in which she uttered the words were as if she was trying to warn Susan.

"Thomas and his deceased wife used to live up that mountain facing down at Waghi," said Martha, thoughtfully. "They were both young at that time, a new couple so eager to start a life together, so they decided to move away from everyone here and moved over there."

"You mean the lonely mountain where Dua stays?" Susan asked.

"Yes. That one." Martha answered, looking directly at Susan. "While they lived there, Thomas often travelled to Lae every two or three weeks to purchase Buai and Coconuts which they resell at Kundiawa Town's main market. The wife is left home alone up that mountain for two or three days until her husband returns, she never goes anywhere when Thomas travels."

"It must have been awfully lonely for her."

"I know, right." Martha said. "Anyways, one morning as usual the wife was still asleep when Thomas took off early in the morning on his usual trip to Lae. But a strange thing happened; Thomas returned back about mid-day the same day. When she enquired why Thomas hadn't travelled to Lae that day Thomas told her that he had thought about it and realised he needed to spend more time with her; it was rather unusual for the wife since Thomas was never a romantic kind of guy. "

"You can say that again." Susan thought out loud. Martha paused and stared at her.

"Should I continue?" Martha asked, annoyed.

"Please, continue Martha."

"After three days the wife was ill. She was too weak to move around. She sat outside the house that afternoon and saw Thomas approaching. Strangely, Thomas came with three local boys who were assisting him bringing in bags of Buai and Coconuts. The wife was instantly taken aback. She had been with Thomas this whole time, Thomas never went to Lae. Thomas could see that his wife was startled and genuinely frightened to receive him. Something was strangely amiss that afternoon. When Thomas stood in front and asked her how she was during the last three days he had left her and travelled to Lae the wife felt her world spun and she collapsed."

Susan fought hard to remain focused. "I'm sorry, I'm not following here."

"Susan, Thomas's first wife had been tricked by a Masalai. For two days it wasn't Thomas she was sleeping with, it was something else. All along Thomas's young wife had been under the impious scrutiny of the evil entity that lurked around that mountain. When the wife was unguarded, the Masalai manifested itself in the guise of Thomas." Susan didn't expect to hear anything like that. She understood the people around Wara Simbu were big on folktales about Masalai love stories and seductions which they found to be sexually invigorating, but Susan wasn't buying any of that.

Susan realised she was wasting her precious time. Martha was obviously consumed with superstitious beliefs and was searching for answers to her own questions in the far unknown. Susan needed a rational human being to talk to. She stood up to leave.

"It breaks my heart but I should probably get going -"

"Agatha had a baby before she hanged herself."

"What?"

"Thomas's deceased wife. Her name was Agatha."

"What happened to the baby?"

"The baby was raised by Thomas's mother - my mother."

"Where is the baby now?"

Martha chuckled, "Well, he's not so much of a baby now as you have already seen."

"Who?"

"Dua. Dua is the son Agatha had right before she killed herself." said Martha. "Thomas wanted nothing to do with Dua after Agatha died. Thomas abandoned Dua when he was just two weeks old, he left Dua to die up in that mountain. If my mother hadn't showed up, Dua would have died. Thomas told everyone later that he was only giving the child back to the real father."

Susan stared at Martha, "you mean the Masalai?"

"Apparently. Thomas is capable of cruel things. It runs in the family, our eldest brother paid the price for cruelty dearly."

"Your eldest brother?"

"Yes. The one before Thomas."

"Does Dua know?"

"I'm not sure. Maybe you should ask him yourself." Martha said.

<h1 style="text-align:center">Chapter 26</h1>

The police car rolled pass Wara Simbu Bridge. The unconscious man had awoken on the floor facing the door at the back of the police ten-seater. Four police men occupied each corner of the back cabin bench comfortably keeping an eye on him. Nem lit up his monster brus, puffed and stared absently out his window at the passing scenery as the Land Cruiser came around a bend.

There was nothing Nem could have done at Numinma, the raid was called off, all he had to do now was work with whatever he had. Vendors at Wara Simbu stood with apprehension as the convoy drove past them without stopping. No raid today. Carry on, Nem thought.

Nem looked up at the mirror and had a flash back on the kind of people that have been brought inside this vehicle; battered and disfigured, they would sit shirtless on the floor facing the door, the perfect lining of spine and ribs glimmer through their light brown skin, their shoulders protruding upwards towering over their heads which hung down in submission showing the spinal lumps at the back of their necks.

From the back anyone could tell how bony, wretched and miserable some of them looked. Nem thought of the first time he had worked as a Policeman in Southern Highlands. A badly disfigured man was brought in on a stormy night, the man sat shirtless shivering at the corner of the questioning room.

Nem was on his night shift when he noticed the man being interrogated under the harsh scrutiny of a rooky officer. Nem paused for a moment just in time as the man looked up. In that brief moment, Nem could see in his eyes; fear and utter hopelessness.

Nem was troubled that night. He couldn't help but feel a deep sense of pity for that man. The final look on the man's face tormented Nem all throughout the night. Nem's own conscious stood him on trial and Nem saw himself guilty; guilty of deliberately neglecting someone who could really use his help.

Still troubled with the image Nem went home. That night Nem couldn't sleep so he snuck back into the station and did everything he could under his power to have that man released. Illegally. The next day Nem learnt that the man he had helped released was a serial rapist and a murderer. Nem was terminated on the spot. Nem couldn't forgive himself. It took him a very long time to clear his record. In a society where the worst kinds of animals could blend in made his job all the more complicated. From that day onwards Nem has taught himself not to be gullible, trust or show mercy to any law breakers. There are wolves in sheep's clothing everywhere. Nem took a lung full of his brus, deep in his own thoughts as the Land Cruiser climbed up Prenoroqwa hill with less effort compared to the PMV busses and container trucks.

"Much ado about nothing." Nem said, absently. The driver couldn't help but ask. "Pardon me?"

Nem looked at the driver, perplexed, he wasn't aware he had said something. "Did you say something?" The driver asked.

"What did I say?" "Much ado about something?"

Nem chuckled, "nothing. Much ado about nothing." Nem said. "Yesterday night we created a big fuss, today we also created a big fuss. All for what? The people we are looking for have been watching us the whole time. That's what it means - too much fuss about nothing."

The driver looked confused. "Boss, I'm not following you."

"The men we are after have been using the mountains to their advantage." Nem said. "They coordinate via mobile phones; they can see us coming from miles away and signal each other."

"That figures." The driver said.

Nem remained quiet briefly as if organising his thoughts. "When we were in Numinma. I thought I saw something." Nem said.

The driver faced Nem, "What did you see?"

"High up on the western mountain top, I saw a group of men watching us," said Nem "I know it's them. I just know. My hunches are never wrong."

"We only need to identify them boss. If we know who they are we can keep an eye out for them." The driver said, trying to sound helpful.

"We already know who they are." Nem said, frankly. "We just need to figure out where they are."

The driver shot a confused look; "you know them already? When were you planning to tell me?" The driver remained quiet, he was new on the job he obviously needed more time to understand and cope with Nem.

Nem's crew runs their business on a 'need to know basis', if you didn't need to know Nem will not tell you. Nem's demeanour and voice is street, but his language is precise like an engineer's. His crew don't do regular policing, Nem has taught them how to blend in with thugs, the only way to catch the bad guys is to think like one, but not to deviate from the course. In his career as a police man, Nam has had the privilege of meeting some of the worst kind of people in PNG often in most unfortunate circumstances, some of them turn out to be good friends with Nem later on in life, the 'demons who turned angels', the police insiders who rat out everyone.

Nem had spent nearly all his life in the company of such men so that to dismiss them altogether would mean taking a big part of his life away.

Chapter 27

Ialasam Gelma materialised on the mountaintop from the east and advanced with the intensity of a panther stalking its prey. His hollow eyes scanned the area as he entered.

Empty. Ialasam Gelma paced forward, his head stood out against the upturned collar of his black leather jacket, his eyes fixated on the open door….. the open door to the hamlet which Dua forgot to lock before he ran down to Waghi in search of his grandmother.

Ialasam approached the hollowness of the open door and glided inside like a snake and disappeared. Moments later he emerged again with a broken piece of mirror in his right hand.

On the southern Cliffside, Oscar and his band of thieves descended down, picking their way through the jutting rocks. Oscar led the way followed by Al Simon, Dei Kembol, and the Rento Brothers trailing behind; always together, side by side.

Jim Rento fished in his bag and offered his brother Mikes a bottle of water, "Thanks so much little brother I really needed this." Mikes said, sounding grateful. "After this job, you and I are going to Moresby. We need to lay low for a while."

Jim nodded with approval. "That's exactly what I was thinking."

Mike regarded his brother Jim as he took his drink. After drinking he gave some back to his brother, "If anything happens to me, I want you go to Moresby and find my daughter." Said Mike. "She must be twelve or thirteen now. Give my share to her mother – "

"Hey, nothing is going to happen." Jim cuts in, rudely. "We have done this kind of job a thousand times. We will go and see your daughter together. Stop talking rubbish." Mike didn't argue, he kept picking his way down without a word. The Rento brothers have never been separated; they have a bond rarely found in brothers.

Al Simon followed Oscar close by. "The way things are going now. After this job we disappear for good. I hope your guy is good." Said Simon.

"Exactly...My guy is good...trust me." Said Oscar as he kept moving.

"How do you know him?"

"I met him a couple of years ago in Kainantu. Kemuti introduced him to me."

"Wait, you mean Kemuti as in 'Old Man' Kemuti?"

"The very same. Told me he was his boy."

"I didn't know Kemuti had a son?"

Oscar stopped walking. "He's not his real son." Said Oscar. "Kemuti trusts him, that's what it means. If Kemuti trusts him... then he's good enough."

Al Simon scratched his head.

Oscar continued moving. "Kemuti told me he took him in when he was very young." Oscar went on. "So basically, he's more like Kemuti's adopted son.....I only saw him probably one or two times, after which I was arrested so I never saw him again."

"Until now." Said Simon. "So, I was right?"

"How do you mean?"

"He is technically Kemuti's son." Al Simon said almost defiantly. Oscar heaved a heavy sigh. This was typical Al Simon, he will always find a way to get even. Al Simon could race a car by foot if he was prancing along and thought the driver overtook him on purpose.

"Yeah, you could say that." Said Oscar, trying not to argue.

"How did you find him now?" Al Simon prodded.

"I didn't find him." Oscar said, facing Al Simon. "He found me."

"What's his name?"

Before Oscar could answer a sharp blinding light struck his face like lightning. Oscar turned away repulsively. The light zigzagged like a fish and rested on Al Simon's chest before moving to Dei Kembol's face. Dei Kembol looked away and muttered a curse to whoever it was that was reflecting the mirror from the eastern mountaintop.

"I'm going to kill that person." Al Simon declared.

"Not so fast." Said Oscar. "That would be my contact's signal." The five men now had arrived precisely at where the contact had sent the signal. They stood side by side with their eyes fixated sceptically at the hamlet. The hollow open door was less inviting.

"This house looks about a hundred years old," said Dei Kembol.

"No doubt," Oscar added.

"Do people still live here?"

"Looks like it." Oscar replied.

"Why would anyone want to live all the way up here?"

"Let's just burn this house." Al Simon jumped in impatiently.

"And attract attention? No way." Oscar said, thoughtfully. "We could use this house for tonight."

"You can't be serious? I'm not going inside that house. Looks like somebody died in there." Said Dei Kembol. "Something doesn't feel right about this place."

"Let's just burn the house." Al Simon said again, sounding edgy.

"Enough with the burning of the house! We are not burning anything!" Oscar snapped.

"What's with you and burning houses?"

"Burn what house?" An alien voice intruded from the back, unannounced.

The gang abruptly turned around in unison. In their line of work, it was mandatory to be on alert, but this time they were caught completely off guard. The startled men came face to face with Ialasam Gelma. Al Simon drew out his gun immediately. "Who the hell are you? Start talking or you're dead."

"Me? Dead? If I wanted you dead, you would be dead already." Ialasam Gelma confronted them in an uncompromising stature, fearless, surveying and scanning each one of their faces carefully.

Oscar pressed down Al Simon's raised gun. "Cool it Sai. This here, is my contact."

Al Simon regarded Ialasam. "You shouldn't sneak up like that. Word of advice."

"My apologies." Said Ialasam as he moved closer. "I didn't mean to startle you. But we have an issue to discuss." The gang convened around Ialasam to listen. "Looks like Christmas came sooner than we anticipated." Ialasam announced, looking at Oscar. "I was informed by my source inside the bank that if we are going pull this bank job, it has to be done no later than tomorrow."

"Tomorrow?" Dei Kembol did a double take.

"Yes. Tomorrow, or never."

"That's insane."

"My initial response." Said Ialasam. "But, wait till you hear this." Ialasam Gelma begin conveying the information he had acquired earlier from John at Dogor. The gang listened attentively without interruptions. When Ialasam Gelma finished talking there was a ripple.

"Three point five million kina?" Dei Kembol did another double take, "Okay, now I really want to rob this bank."

Oscar raised his hand to silence his men. "Run us through the exit plan." Ialasam Gelma rifled in his jacket and produced a paper.

"The exit plan follows a tight schedule. This is to say the robbery goes smoothly without any disturbances. The exit plan can only accommodate success, there is no plan 'B', any delay or failure will ultimately compromise our exit plan. In such instance every man will be for himself." Said Ialasam. "If the robbery goes smoothly, we will have roughly thirty minutes open window, and at least two to three hours head start."

"When you said 'open window' you mean the time we walk out of the bank with the money and leave Kundiawa Town right?" Oscar asked.

"Yes. And that's saying the play goes smoothly."

"And the two to three hours head start?"

"That's when we are already in Omkolai, by than the police would have already been alerted so we would then have a two to three hours head start. We will ditch the car and travel by foot all the way around Sine Sine and resurface in Chuave. From Chuave I have already arranged someone to pick us up from that point to Goroka. In Goroka we are home free."

"Don't you think the exit plan maybe a bit too predictable?" Oscar asked, trying not to sound discourteous. "How are you so sure the highway patrol will not be waiting for us in Chuave?"

"I realised this trend, which is why I have my men there in Omkolai. They will take the car from where we left and go to

Gumuni or wherever they want to, it's really not our problem from there on." Said Ialasam. "Once the police are diverted from us, nobody is going to bother checking Chuave. While everyone is looking for us in Gumuni, we would already be in Eastern Highlands."

"The cost of bringing in Extra men will come from your cut." Dei Kembol said. "No one told you to bring in extras."

Ialasam shot Kembol a defiant look. "You think you can waltz up to their village with three point five million kina without acknowledging them?"

"He's right." Oscar added. "We can't go past without running by them first. A bit of loose change from three point five million won't matter. I will gladly chip in."

"Thank you." Said Ialasam. "The exit plan looks set. Now let's hear how exactly we are going to make this play." Oscar asked.

Everyone was facing Ialasam. In all seriousness. Ialasam took a whiff of the humid air before speaking. "This has never been done before. No crew is stupid or crazy enough to pull it off. Which is why this will be one of the riskiest jobs you will ever do. There is no guarantee that we will survive this. In the event that something goes wrong, things will be very ugly for all of us."

"How do you suppose we go pass the security, not to mention a jammed packed town with the police station nearby without raising the alarm? It will be like walking into a bee hive." Kembol asked.

"I realised that. That's why we will go in with the Queen bee. They won't know they are robbed until it's too late." Said Ialasam.

"Who is the Queen bee?" Al Simon had to ask.

"The bank manager." Oscar answered, flatly. "Large-scale cash robbery was once a technical challenge. Today, the weak points in the banks are not grilles and vaults, but human beings. This is psychology. It will not take gelignite to blow up the vault; but fear. How the bank manager would respond if his family were in mortal danger."

"Tiger kidnapping." Dei Kembol added.

"Precisely. This is where old-fashioned crime meets modern terrorism. It will be a new chapter in the tale of cops and robbers. A theft tailor-made for the twenty first century." Oscar said, theatrically.

"What is the vault's design?" Dei Kembol asked.

"It's round. The door's round." Said Ialasam. "This unique design of round vault doors makes them highly secure. Their operation hinges on a balance of mechanical engineering and security technology, ensuring that only authorised personnel can gain access. It has a dual control system, meaning that two authorized individuals must be present to access the vault, enhancing security."

"The main vault?" Kembol asked.

"No, the main gate to the bank's premises. Off course I'm talking about the main vault here." Ialasam answered, irritated. "This main vault requires two people to access. The teller vaults require one person to access. We are interested in the main vault. The main vault has an outer door which requires two people to open and then inner doors which require the same two people to open. It has a dual control system, meaning, as I have said; two authorised individuals must be present to access the vault."

"It has to be the bank manager and someone else. While a bank manager may have the ability to access a vault during regular hours, accessing it after hours would involve significant security measures and protocols that make it much less likely and more difficult." Said Oscar.

"That's right." Ialasam concurred. "That's why we have to go in and wait for the bank to open with the bank manager. We will go together with him when the bank is open and pull this off."

"Who has the other combination?" Oscar asked.

"A senior bank taller by the name of Maria Bonge," Ialasam said, "she lives up at the Premieres Hill. We will pick her up on our way to the bank. The bank manager will make that arrangement. She will not know anything until she is inside the car with us. Got it?" Oscar nodded knowingly. "Listen Ialasam." Said Oscar. "This play can be a five man show. We are proficient the way we are right now. I want you to keep an eye on the bank manager's family while we make play."

"I don't have any problems with that. As long as it gets the job done right." Ialasam said.

"Good. Very good. Tonight, the play commences. We take the bank manager before dawn." Said Oscar.

"Everything goes down tonight." Ialasam looked directly at Oscar before shifting his gaze, in that brief moment Oscar could have sworn he thought Ialasam Gelma was someone else.

Chapter 28

I alasam Gelma led the gang down to Waghi river. When they arrived at the riverside, he told them to wait for him and he disappeared.

"Seems like a nice guy," Al Simon said after Ialasam had gone out of sight.

"I think I've seen him somewhere, I can't quite remember where exactly."

"You must have seen him in Goroka." Oscar added. "He grew up there, or so I've heard."

Dei Kembol took a seat on a tree log, sighing. "Ialasam? What kind of stupid name is that? His name sounds weird. Never heard a name more profoundly stupid as that."

"And you think yours is better?" Al Simon said, sounding defensive. "Let me ask you a question, and please answer it truthfully so we can all hear. What do you call a woman's private part in Western Highlands?"

Dei Kembol suddenly seemed uneasy with that question. He wasn't sure how he was going to answer that. But he looked around and saw that everyone was eagerly waiting for his response. He was hesitant. "Well, I – ah…when I was little – "

"Hey, I didn't ask for a life story." Al Simon prodded. "Just simply answer the question bro."

"Alright fine, they call it kemb." Die Kembol said, embarrassed. "A woman's private part is called kemb in Western Highlands."

A hoarse laughter erupts by the riverside. On the far side of that river bank Dua immediately swings around alarmed by the laughter. Dua gets to his feet and scans his surroundings. He could see Mona swinging her tail from side to side enjoying the lush vegetation along the river banks. He looked to his left and saw Grandma deep in her own thoughts under a tree shade.

Dua fixed his gaze on Grandma and felt a sense of guilt. He knew Grandma would not talk to him for a long time after the obscene spectacle he pulled off with Robin earlier. What was that? Dua couldn't believe he had done such a thing, that sure as hell was not me! He thought. He felt like he was possessed. He couldn't possibly bring himself to it. He was embarrassed, not knowing if he would have the courage to confront Robin and apologise.

"What I did was shameful." Dua thought out loud.

"What's shameful?" Ialasam Gelma intruded from the back in an alien cadence. Dua swung around and felt his heart racing fast.

"What's shameful Dua?" Ialasam asked.

"I did something today which I was not supposed to do. I am ashamed of my actions." Dua said, truthfully.

"That's alright Dua, we all make mistakes. But you must learn not to repeat that same mistake again." Ialasam said. "How is your grandmother doing? I hope she is not ashamed of what she tried to do to me last night. I forgive her. I mean it."

Dua glanced over at Grandma. "She's over there, you can tell her yourself. But I'm not sure she wants to talk to anyone today. She is still mad at me." Said Dua.

"That's ok, let her be. I need a favour from you." Dua gave an apprehensive look at Ialasam.

"What is it?"

"I have guests with me. I need to give them a feast before they depart. Call it the last supper." Said Ialasam, sarcastically. "I'm going to need that juicy fat pig of yours to kill for my friends."

"No. I will not let you harm Mona." Dua said, defiantly. "Go ask someone else."

"Don't make this hard on yourself. I'm trying to be nice here. If you won't allow me, I will kill that pig myself in front of you while you stand and watch. Don't test me."

"I won't allow it!"

Ialasam drew out his pistol. "Suit yourself Dua. I wasn't asking." Ialasam walked over casually to the spot where Mona was grazing; held out his gun, took a dead aim on the pig's head and shot the animal square on the temple without hesitation. Mona fell over. Dead. Grandma screamed with horror. Dua fell on his knees with disbelief.

"You are insane! Why are you doing this to me?" Ialasam wasn't paying attention to the wailing and complaining, he pulled the animal carcass by the front hoofs across the sand; a predator dragging it's kill into the bush and out of sight.

Dua rose up from the dirt with boiling rage and storms after Ialasam. Ialasam moved very quickly through the bushes dragging his kill along. He was fast. He finally surfaces around the corner coming into full view of the gang. The men rejoiced when they saw him dragging the animal carcass along.

Dua suddenly came to an abrupt halt, and stood shrouded in the bushes when he saw men with guns coming forward assisting Ialasam bringing in the kill. They all looked ecstatic.

Dua realised it would be wise not to interfere. These were bad looking men in every sense of the word. Dua stood shrouded in the bushes and witnessed helplessly as Al Simon surgically removed Mona's gut with a sharp blade. The rest of the gang stood around and watched considerately. Occasionally Oscar would remark at how efficient Simon is, and Simon would glimmer under his perspiration.

Dua felt bitter inside, yet he could do nothing but watch. These men know not reasoning nor shame, it would be fatal if he attempts to interfere when they are in the middle this ceremony. He gulped down all his rage and watched.

All the effort, and all the time Dua had invested into protecting, taking care, and fattening up the pig meant nothing now. The devourers usually think little and have no appreciation of the hands that raised the livestock Dua thought. As Dua watched, Oscar lit up a cigarette and spoke, "It's been a while since I've eaten a pig, the demon in me is hungry and impatient, I'm starting up the fire."

Oscar cut out from the group, but stopped when Kembol enquired how exactly the pig's meat was to be cooked.

"We slice the meat to pieces and roast them." Oscar said.

Kembol looked slightly disappointed, "I was thinking more along the line of a pit mumu"

"It will be a waste of time."

"He's right," Simon looked up from where he knelt. "We don't have time; I'm just going to slice the meat to roast small size pieces."

"Very well, do as you wish." Kembol observed, thoughtfully. "It is such a shame to see a quality pig meat like this treated with disrespect. The least you ingrates can do is show some courteous appreciation for the bounty which you lot least deserve."

Chapter 29

"This is the best thing I have eaten in my life." Dei Kembol said as he hacked into the huge chunk of crispy pork meat. A mixture of juice and blood trickled down his overgrown beard.

"I thought you prefer pit-mumu?" Asked Oscar.

"I did...but I changed my mind."

"I myself prefer meat with a little bit of blood," said Oscar. "Pit-mumu sucks the fun out of it, wouldn't you agree?"

Dei Kembol nodded his head while munching into the meat, savagely. Oscar thought he looked like a hungry lion.

Oscar turned his attention back to the dark crispy slab of meat sitting on the dry log in front of him. He pulled out his knife, sliced a small piece, stabbed that piece with the knife and raised it up. He then carefully inspected the meat before devouring it.

There was silence all around, a hexagon of silence as all six men got busy eating. A rare feast as such had the way of commanding the attention of men, even the uncanny. It is the one time all men try to be civilized.

Al Simon produced salt out of nowhere and started seasoning his share of crispy ribs. The others immediately turned at the sound and groaned. "Oh c'mon! You had the salt the whole time?"

"But no one asked." Al Simon replied. Dei Kembol regretted he had consumed too much flavourless pork already. Nonetheless, he considered what was left of his share and waited for the salt to go around.

"Where did you get that salt?" Oscar asked.

"It's mine. I bought it." Al Simon said, almost defensively.

"You bought it?"

"Yeah, I bought it. I don't steal salt."

"When did you buy it?"

"I bought it in Goroka before we came here."

Oscar tightened his gaze. "You mean the salt was with you for the last three weeks?"

"Yeah. I was saving it for this." Al Simon replied flatly. A hoarse laughter erupted. Jim Rento smiled for the first time, watching him laugh was like witnessing a solar eclipse, it was hideously beautiful.

Dei Kembol was gasping for air but managed. "What kind of man carries a salt around?"

"It's better to have one and not need it than to need one and not have it." Replied Al Simon. "Just like condoms."

"Don't tell me you have condoms too."

"As a matter of fact I do." Al Simon replied as he riffled in his back pocket and produced three lubricated condoms linked together in silver pack. The hoarse laughter increased in volume.

Ialasam Gelma observed in silence, barely touching his pork. The scum of the earth dines, and talk about condoms and salt how lovely, he thought. As the laughter subdued Oscar turned to Ialasam.

"Say Ialasam...are there any beautiful girls left in Wara Simbu?"

"Left? Last I checked they never left." Said Ialasam. The question was random and Ialasam wasn't sure if he had answered right.

"When was the last time you checked?" Oscar asked, candidly.

Ialasam noticed the rest of the gang were also keen on hearing his answer. There was no point lying to these men, they can smell a lie quicker than shit. "Last night." Answered Ialasam truthfully.

"Who was she?"

"She was a married woman. I just borrowed her for the night."

"Where was the husband?"

"He was up the road busy with the police. She was down by the riverside busy with me. We all got busy. It was busy night." Replied Ialasam frankly. The rest of the gang chuckled. They seem to be enjoying this. But Oscar still couldn't help noticing that strangeness in Ialasam.....there was no human emotion.

Oscar couldn't place it. He silenced Al Simon who wanted Ialasam to explain in detail about the steamy affair. Somethings are better left unsaid. Oscar turned to face everyone, "We will lay low here until midnight," said Oscar, seriously. "By twelve midnight we go up to Kipre, and take the round down to Talis, and all the way down to the Bank Manager's residence. After we take the Manager and his family hostage, we will stay with them until dawn. By seven, we will ride with him to the bank."

Oscar turns to face Ialasam, "As for you my friend," said Oscar. "You will stay with the family until the play is done. You will walk out of there at nine to meet us at the rendezvous. Don't be late. But, if anything happens to us up there, you're on your own pal."

Ialasam nodded, "Understood. Loud and clear."

Sixty miles away, a PMV bus comes to a stop at Migin Chuave District. The locals paused from whatever they were doing to see which one of their relatives would arrive this late in the afternoon.

Gigmai hopped out of the bus to a throng of inquisitive stares. He is a troublemaker; the last thing he needed was someone whom he pissed off from way back walking up to him.

Four burly young men in their mid-twenties stood beside the roadside looking directly at Gigmai. The four men were smoking, Gigmai could smell marijuana in the air. That's not good, Gigmai thought. He forced a nervous smile, surprisingly the men smiled back and waved.

One of the young men broke out from the pack and walked towards Gigmai. He was huge, at least 6"2 and very broad. He smiled as he came near,

"Hey, I remember you from Wara Simbu, I came to your house and bought kambe." Said the young man, smiling.

Gigmai immediately felt a sense of dread, the guy had a very imposing stature, and deep penetrating dark eyes. Gigmai definitely wouldn't cross him.

Gigmai summoned his last ounce of courage, "Oh that's right! I remember you small bro," said Gigmai, lying. "Your name is Joe – Josh, or was it Josef?"

"My name's Brian," said the young man, flatly. "That's right, Brian, I was gonna say that. I remember you, you're my favourite customer," said Gigmai, lying again. "How are you doing?"

"I'm good, what brings you here this late? Visiting someone?"

"Yes I am, I'm here to see my good friend Masane," said Gigmai. "He told me to come, I know it's awfully late but – " Brian's facial reaction changed. Gigmai realised automatically that didn't look good, "Perhaps I might be in the wrong place – "

"No. You are in the right place." Said Brian.

"Alright. Perhaps you could point me to his house?"

"You want to see him?"

"Yes, yes, I want to see him. It's important that I do."

"Sure, I will take you to him."

"That will be wonderful, thank you so much."

"Follow me, and don't call him by that name," said Brian, seriously. "You're lucky you saw me first, I'm his nephew. If you had seen the other guys they would have belted you up just for calling his name."

Gigmai considered himself lucky and followed Brian. Gigmai doesn't know who Masane is let alone why he needed to see him and deliver the message from Ialasam. Gigmai was always kept in the dark, he had learnt to accept the fact that he was merely Ialasam's errand boy doing his dirty work. To Gigmai, Ialasam was a mysterious character that arrived two months ago and changed his life. Gigmai had never felt he was part of something big until he met Ialasam. Gigmai considered Ialasam a strange character, but for some reason he trusted him.

Initially, Ialasam came to him at an odd hour, it was 4:30 AM in the morning, he gave Gigmai some money and spoke to Gigmai about his outrageous adventures and how easy it is to make a lot of money doing crime, he explained the mechanics of it like an engineer, as odd as it is it was as if the demon inside Gigmai naturally venerated the legions housed inside Ialasam.

Gigmai easily succumbed to Ialasam's overpowering dark influence, now he knows too much to back out. He had to confess that Ialasam had a way of exploiting the slightest darkness he sees in men, it was a gift, a rare one perhaps anointed by the devil himself.

Now as Gigmai was following Brian he thought of that encounter with Ialasam two months ago, and how it had changed his life. He was now following a stranger to meet someone he barely knew. They had walked some distance from the main highway, it was already getting dark and Brian had to use his torch light for guidance.

Brian stopped walking as if sensing Gigmai's uncertainty, "Look, I don't know what trouble you are in, it is really not my business," said Brian. "Maybe you people at Wara Simbu are used to it, but here in Chuave we can smell lies quicker than shit. You have been lying to me the minute you came out of that bus. Now I'm going to ask you frankly, do not lie to me, you are in my territory, I own the air you breath. Tell me why you are here."

Gigmai felt the tension in the atmosphere. Brian wasn't asking, Gigmai knew he had to be honest, "I am sorry small bro," said Gigmai. "I was sent here by a friend of Masane – "

"Who is he? What's his name?"

"His name's Ialasam."

"Ialasam?"

"Yes, that's what I call him."

"That sounds like a stupid made up name."

"I'm telling you the truth."

"Looks like the person who sent you lied about his name."

"That's his name," said Gigmai, struggling. "I'm only here to give a message to Masane. Ialasam told me Masane will know what to do. I'm just the messenger."

Brian didn't respond to Gigmai. He walked a short distance towards a small garden, then he stopped walking and called Gigmai to join him. Gigmai sceptically arrived beside Brian. Gigmai saw Brian looking down at the garden, and Brian cleared his throat, "You said you wanted see Masane and deliver a message?"

"Yes, that's what you heard me say."

"Masane is listening, speak."

"You are Masane?"

"I'm his nephew. Masane is over there," said Brian, pointing his torch light to a grave yard beside the garden. "Masane has been dead for over three years, he was shot to death by Police in Goroka. I don't know what kind of idiot would listen to a complete stranger and follow his instruction all the way here to deliver a message to a dead man," said Brian. "Whoever sent you here tricked you."

Gigmai went pale, a feeling of complete betrayal came over him, he couldn't speak. Ialasam Gelma had fooled him. Gigmai was now caught in a predicament in the dark in another man's land. Going back to Wara Simbu was no longer an option, there will be people looking for him. He was halfway to Goroka already.

Gigmai stood there not knowing what to do or where to go next.

Chapter 30

That evening Thomas Grakumne snuck inside the room and tried to make love to his wife Susan, but she refused blatantly. Thomas tried enticing her with money, "I will give you some money tomorrow so you can go to the Town and buy something nice for yourself," Thomas said.

"What do you say darling?" Susan looked over at Thomas with raw disgust in her eyes, if looks could kill Thomas would probably die right there. Thomas wasn't going to back down easily, he desperately wanted to feel Susan, he produced sixty-four kina from his pocket and offered it to his wife.

"Here, this is all the money in my pocket right now," said Thomas, desperately. "I will get some more money from the store and give it to you later, please I am your husband just let me in, if you don't want to see my face you can cover it with a pillow." Susan almost blurted out laughing, but she adamantly refused to succumb to Thomas. She saw Thomas for who he truly was – a miserable middle aged man without any attraction let alone sex appeal, she wasn't remotely aroused by his doggedness. Thomas can't force her, this was her body.

"I am honestly not in the mood Thomas." Susan said, sincerely. "You can take your money to Rot Kona, there are girls who will gladly give you discount for fifty kina. I really don't mind."

Thomas fumed, "How dare you say something like that, I am a community leader with integrity," said Thomas. "I can't be seen with prostitutes, are you retarded?"

Susan turned over, half serious and saw Thomas on the edge of the bed sulking, you look miserable, Susan thought. Susan was thinking about Ialasam's young athletic body and his rare infectious smile before she was rudely interrupted by Thomas, now as she was watching Thomas complaining her mind drifted off, the thing I would do to Ialasam if it was him right here with me tonight, she thought.

"Are you sleeping around behind my back?" Thomas asked, candidly.

Susan was caught off guard, "What? No, why would you say something like that Thomas?"

"Because I am a seasoned man." Said Thomas. "I have been dealing with women long before you were even born. I know when a woman is sleeping with another man, I can smell the odour of another man on you. Who is he?"

Susan suddenly went cold, for a moment there she thought Thomas had somehow read her mind, but that's impossible. This wasn't the first time Susan had fooled around with Ialasam, Susan and Ialasam had been seeing each other secretly, always in the night time for well over a month now. Thomas never suspected anything, or so Susan thought.

"Thomas, you are just paranoid," said Susan. "Everything you are saying now is just inside your head. Don't trouble yourself."

Thomas sat on the edge of the bed, contemplating. Susan didn't like that. Thomas's silence is usually followed by rage, Susan needed to dissolve that as soon as possible, "Thomas,

I'm your wife, you are the only one entitled to me," said Susan, softly. "I'm just not feeling well tonight –"

"Did Martha tell you what happened to my first wife?" Thomas asked before Susan could finish. Susan nodded her head, "She did, I'm sorry."

"You shouldn't be. She got what she deserved," Thomas said. "She cheated on me with a demon, she couldn't live with herself, so she killed herself. She had an abomination before she died. Did you know what I did to that child?"

"Thomas you are scaring me –"

"You haven't seen what I can actually become if you trigger me correctly," said Thomas. "You'd be delusional if you think that moral dissonance you are having gives you license to make me the problem in your dysfunctional mind."

"Thomas, I am not entitled to it, I belong to you –"

"Stop it please, it's pathetic. If a certain someone has weaved his way into your life, and the more you are starting to believe that you are the victim, and you think that justifies you to seek comfort in someone else's arm, I am going to tell you this," said Thomas, taunting. "The story does not end well for you. That brief feeling of freedom when you are validated by that someone will be the end of you." Thomas stood up and gave one last look at Susan before he walked out.

Susan sat there speechless as Thomas left.

Chapter 31

Damien Tupa awoke from a deep sleep to the relentless barking of the dog outside. The dog's barking had bored into his skull. Damien was more furious than alarmed as he should be, and he immediately regretted buying the puppy in the first place.

Damien rolled over and sat at the edge of his bed in the dark staring blankly out the window. The moon filtered through the bay window and played on the oriental rug. Damien looked over at the table clock and saw the digital numbers 03:36 AM. Going back to bed was useless.

Damien looked over and caught his wife peacefully asleep regardless of the tormenting barking outside. He couldn't keep his eyes to himself; she looked exceedingly beautiful sleeping sideways with her hand in a protective gesture over her swollen tummy. He felt a powerful surge of love overcome him.

She will make a fine mother, she has proven herself worthy with my two daughters already Damien thought. Such is life, when less than three years ago Damien's life had hit the crossroads; at the age of 36 his previous marriage had fallen into the abyss without a glimmer of hope, and he wasn't advancing anywhere after over a decade of working for the bank.

The opportunity to bail out presented itself when he was asked to fill in the vacuum left by the untimely demise of Kundiawa Bank branch manager. It was a huge vacuum, it was what he had been hoping for, and there couldn't have been a better timing. Damien grabbed the opportunity without a second glance and had never looked back since then.

Chimbu was nothing like what he was expecting. The locals made trying to make him fit in seem like an outdated strategy; they treated Damien as if he grew up around the place and was only returning. Damien was treated with a respect he had never known in his life. He found joy in his work again, he also found love, and the best part of all was watching his daughters adapting well and fast. Damien Tupa was whole and complete at last. What could possibly go wrong - The barking outside suddenly came to an halt with a final squeal from the dog. The dog was silenced completely by something or someone.

Damien immediately rose to his feet and walked over to the window. Alarmed. From the master bedroom window upstairs nothing below could be missed that night. The cloudless night sky, and the bright oval moonlight overpowered all earthly lights. Damien could spot a bottle cap laying on the lawn that night.

He let his eyes travel all around the yard for any sign of life. The dog was nowhere to be seen. The trees swayed gracefully and gently to the invisible hand of the wind. There was silence all around. Dead silence.

Damien felt the hair at the back of his neck stand up. His sixth sense was activated, and he instinctively knew something was wrong. Damien tried waking his wife up but she mumbled an innocent curse and passed out again. Damien knew that if he persisted trying to wake her up his whole day could be ruined if she wakes up with a temper and realises it was a false alarm.

Experience had taught him that it is wise never to rattle a pregnant woman.

It's probably nothing serious, the dog must have slipped and fell Damien thought... Wait, slipped and fell? Damien shook his head for cobwebs and walked out of the room to investigate.

What worried Damien the most was the fact that when the dry season started to take its toll, people all around have resorted to eating their own pets. Dog meat topped the El Nino Menu. People had to carry their cats and dogs around for their own safety, leaving their pets home alone was no longer an option.

A moment ago he wanted the dog dead, but now as it weighed on him he regretted that thought. Damien stood in the lounge room downstairs, turned on the light switch, and headed for the main door. Unarmed. He was never a violent man so the thought of grabbing a baseball bat just in case never crossed his mind. Even if he did carry a baseball bat, he could never use it to hurt someone.

Damien unlocked the main door, turned the door knob, and pulled the door wide open. He was greeted by a gush of cold breeze. The night was beautiful; the moon hung low, even more so too, low craters could be seen, patches of mist on mountaintops far out were visible. This was never the case during the rainy seasons, the El Nino was ugly, yes, but on the bright side the nights were divine.

Damien quickly let the beauty of the night slip and quickly returned his attention back to the dog. He paced around the yard calling the dog's name but there was no response from the animal. The pinch of pity inside grew each time he called out the dog's name in vain. If the dog was alive she would respond instantly, she was a very obedient dog, this was the first time Damien had called out her name more than once...and probably the last. Damien felt tears swell up and trickle down.

The dog was gone. Killed and taken away...Damien couldn't bring himself up to it.

People all around were losing their dogs to similar fate, it was only a matter of time before some lunatic got to Damien's. Damien felt terrible as he walked back towards the house to go inside. "I should have let her sleep inside the house." Damien said to himself as he walked looking around. He cursed himself.

Damien stopped in front of the door to have one last look around the yard. Silence. Motionless. The whole universe was asleep. The dog was gone and there was nothing he could do at the moment except retire back and hope.

Damien contemplated how he would even begin to explain the situation to his daughters. He would have to alert his wife first, and report the matter to the police in the morning, in the meantime he had to work on an explanation for his daughters. He will have to put a police report but the police won't do anything! Damien thought.

Children were dying from starvation all around Chimbu Province, human beings were missing, the chances of the police taking the case of a missing dog was very slim.

Damien ran this through his mind as he turned to walk inside, but he stopped short when he noticed a five kina (K5) note laying there on the welcome home rug at his feet.

That's odd, Damien thought. Frowning he bent down to pick up the money, as he did so an enormous shadow cast from inside the house blotted out the light, aghast Damien immediately retracted and came face to face with Ialasam Gelma who was aiming his pistol directly on Damien's face.

"Shh don't make a sound or your end will be swift." Whispered Ialasam, maleficently.

Damien gasped. His body trembled all over. The feeling of a complete stranger aiming a gun at him was terrifying in every sense of the word. Damien didn't realise that he had pissed his pants. Oscar materialised behind Ialasam.

"I hope you don't mind Damien. We let ourselves in." Said Oscar.

Before Damien could process how these strangers knew him, and what the hell was going on two other men came from behind and shoved him inside the house.

Chapter 32

Damien Tupa's wife Anna had awoken in a twilight state. Her eyes partly shut, while her brain did a reality check. She was in a blurred intersection trying to figure out if the voices she was hearing were real or not. The muffled voices merged with her faded dreams and formed a meaningless coloration. She could only hear woozy prattling.

Suddenly, her brain surged a powerful wave throughout her being, forcing her to sit upright. She glanced around in darkness dazed. Damien wasn't where he should be. She adjusted her ears and heard muffled voices coming from downstairs through the open bedroom door.

She dragged her gaze across to the bedside table and saw the digital numbers '04:50' registered on the clock. What's going on? She felt a rising anger at Damian for entertaining visitors at this time of the night; it couldn't have been anyone else at this hour except his drinking buddies.

She dragged herself out of bed without a sound and tiptoed out the room. Along the corridor a cocky idea materialised. She stopped moving. Then she smiled inside at the thought of giving their visitors a fright, at this hour it would be priceless, she thought.

She couldn't help the smile on her face either. She suppressed the laughter and tiptoed towards the illuminated varnished stairwell from the light downstairs. She couldn't help it, it had to be done.

When she reached the stairwell, she could hear that the voices downstairs were all unfamiliar. The smile was erased from her face. She slowly descended down the stairway trying her best to be discrete. When she arrived downstairs, she could see her husband inside the kitchen, sitting down on the chair motionless, with his hands on his lap, facing the blindside at the opposite end of the dining table listening to someone.

Whoever her husband was listening to suddenly stopped talking as if he or she had sensed Anna's presence. Anna did not move. Female intuition was a potent instinct that she had learned to trust, and something was wrong she could tell.

"Damian?" Anna called over, "Is everything alright." Damien turned slowly to face his wife. Anna thought he looked like a ghost. Anna knew her husband well enough to understand that the look on his face was one of fear, deep rotting fear. She had never seen him like that before.

"Damian what is going on?" Anna called over again, she was afraid to go any closer.

Damian turned back to face the blind side, whoever was there spoke in a barely audible tone this time. After listening, Damian slowly turned his head towards Anna again, this time he looked paler and sicker.

Anna felt a mixture of anxiety and rage bubbling up inside. "Damian Tupa!" Anna roared. "What the fu-" A broad palm clamped hard over her mouth, yanking her back. Instantly, a powerful arm was wrapped around her torso, pinning her against a rock-hard chest.

For a split second, Anna went numb with shock. Then came the terror. She fought, trying to twist away, but she was no match for the man's size and strength. She tried to scream, but his hand remained tightly across her mouth.

He leaned down and placed his mouth next to her ear, whispering, "Shhh sister calm down, when I take my hand off your mouth, you will not scream, is that clear?"

She nodded vigorously, her lungs burning for air. I can't breathe! She could hear Damian pleading for her life over the sound of her own heartbeat. The man removed his hand from her mouth, and Anna gasped, inhaling deeply.

"That's it sister, I won't hurt you," the man said. Anna was escorted towards Damien. She was fighting to maintain her composer.

Damian what the hell is going on?

Chapter 33

Anna looked over and saw Damian sobbing. Suddenly another man materialised behind Damian with a rifle in hand. Gradually like snakes venturing out into the open, two other man slowly come out from the blind corner and the three men converged around Damian, before she could process any of their faces another man walked past Anna without warning, Anna gasped with horror.

Oh my God! Was he just upstairs? Anna looked around and saw in the living room that someone else had been sitting on the couch and watching the whole time.

There are strange men all over my house! An icy fear churned in her gut. Anna felt totally at a loss. Who are these people – She felt the powerful hand on her shoulder ushering her forward. Anna complied without protest. She was too shock stricken to resist.

When she arrived at the kitchen one of the men pulled out the chair next to Damian and motioned Anna to sit. Anna took the seat without a word. She glanced over and saw Damian still sobbing, she felt a pinch of pity laced with anger.

She understood Damian was not a violent man, she never held that against him, but she also knew herself very well that if she was not seven months pregnant she would have put up a fight with these men before they took her down, Damian had no excuse she thought.

"Now that we are all acquainted let's get to it," said Oscar, finally. "We are not here to hurt you or your family, trust me. We are only here for a small favour as I have already spoken with your husband while you were still asleep."

Anna turned to face Damian. Damian seemed distant, as if he was sort of hoping this was all a bad dream. Anna summoned her courage,

"What do you want from us?" Anna asked, almost causally.

"Good question." Said Oscar. "What I want from you is to remain here with your two daughters who are upstairs, while me and your husband go for a ride in the morning. Can you do that?"

Anna shot a confused stare at Damian. Damian was still in his distant mode.

Oscar rifled in his pocket and produced a cell phone, "Okay, the time is now almost five sharp." Said Oscar, "We have less than two hours to kill, at six thirty, me and some of my men will follow Damian to work. Damian will conceal all this, and he will try not to do anything out of the ordinary, is that right Damian?"

Damian nodded without a word. Anna could only watch. Oscar slid the cell phone back.

"We know your routine Damian, so if anything strikes us as amiss, for instance you try to do something out of the ordinary.....your family will be killed, including the unborn child, think about it." Oscar said. "We will let you live to regret it."

Damian stared at Oscar, "I will do anything you want," Damian said. "Just leave my family out of this."

"Wise words," said Oscar. "The night is darkest just before dawn, in less than an hour the sun rises, but your night will linger on for all eternity if you fail me."

Anna still couldn't see where all these was going. It took her a while to finally figure out why these men were here, then it finally dawned on her, oh my God, these guys are going to rob the Kundiawa Bank! Anna thought.

"Coffee?" Al Simon appeared without warning beside her, holding a tray of steaming coffee with biscuits. "I thought you might like some." Anna wasn't sure if she was going to thank Al Simon or not. This was her coffee inside her house being served by a complete stranger.

Apparently, Al Simon had made himself well at home and started serving coffee and biscuits to everyone. Anna made a quick glance around while taking her coffee and saw that most of the men were in their late thirties and early forties. They were all armed with high powered rifles, poised and exuberant, they didn't show as nervous.

Anna identified Oscar as the leader; he was calculated and composed, his eyes radiated intelligence, and the rest of the gang seem to draw their energy from him. Bravery and stupidity couldn't sum up this gang.

Raised in a military background Anna could tell the difference between bad ass and wannabe bad ass, one thing Anna was certain of was that this gang was the real deal, and it was in her best interest to comply.

Oscar took his coffee and placed it on the table, "So, how long have you two's been married?"

The question startled Anna, she glanced over at Damien, "T-two years..."

"Two years?"

"Yes."

"And the girls upstairs? They are from Damien's previous marriage?"

"Yes."

Oscar sipped his coffee and switched his regard to Damien, "You were married before with two daughters, what happened? Why did you bail out?"

Damien suddenly felt uneasy. He could feel Anna's eyes on him. "I-I did what I had to."

"But you still haven't answered my question. Was it her fault? Because you seem like a decent man?" Damien hated to be reminded about his past, but this guy was prodding with a machine gun, what choice did he have?

"Yes, I guess it was her fault," said Damien.

"You guess? What were you doing at that time? Uncertain about life? Why did you leave her? Did she dump you?" Oscar prodded.

"I left her. I just left." Said Damien, barely fighting back his emotions. Oscar took another sip of his coffee and lit up a cigarette, he took a lung full, exhaled, and reclined back,

"She cheated on you, did she? It's written all over your face." Damien felt the night shattered. All the memories he had worked hard to blot out from his mind reared into his head again. "Did you beat her up?" Oscar asked.

Damien shook his head. "She wasn't worth it."

"Oh c'mon! Surely you must have done something?"

"I didn't do anything." Said Damien, weakly. There are laws in place moron, you obviously have no idea about that! Damian thought to himself. Oscar shook his head disappointedly. The rest of the gang converged and watched. Sipping their coffee.

Anna fought hard to supress the boiling anger at the pit of her stomach.

Ialasam Gelma sipped his coffee away from them and thought of what would happen to Susan if Thomas found out about their affair. He was in his own world.

"If I was you, I'd remarry, just like what you have done." Said Oscar, "Just to get my mind off her, but don't you think it's a little bit selfish to use someone as beautiful and innocent as Anna just to fill the empty space inside left by a heartless woman? Shouldn't you be on a prowl for a single mother who is broken and miserable like yourself? You would have common ground to discuss on marital matters, instead of using a young women who would be better off creating her own dreams rather than living in your gloomy world."

Damien's face now was pale as death. He stared at Oscar incredulous. Why are you tormenting me? Oscar was obviously no ordinary criminal; he broke people both physically and mentally.

"You are a coward Damien," Oscar said, "a miserable coward, the only thing noble and brave that will come from you right now is saving your family. If you fail me now, your life will truly have no purpose."

Oscar saw this side of Damian in two minutes which Anna took two years to figure out. Damian had the tendency to run away from his problems without confronting it, it was the part of him which Anna disliked, yet she never braved the chance to talk about it.

Oscar spoke bluntly as if he had known Damian his whole life, Anna couldn't help but somewhat agree with Oscar. He does have a point though.

Outside the house early birds were chirping. The blue horizon on the mountain tops could be seen from the kitchen window.

Oscar took out his cell phone again and glanced at it, "It's almost time. Go bring down the girls Anna." Said Oscar.

"Follow her Al, in case she tries anything stupid."

Chapter 34

Anna brought her two daughters down escorted by Al Simon.

Al Simon had his gun tucked away, well hidden from the two little girls. The rest of the gang did the same when the girls showed up. They didn't want to terrify them.

The girls were still half asleep, totally unaware of anything. Their innocence added a rather odd touch to the atmosphere.

"Good morning lovely ladies." Oscar said, casually. "You girls hungry? Want something to eat? Come sit down and your mummy will make you breakfast. My name is Peter; you can call me uncle Peter." Oscar lied.

"And the short guy standing next to you is your uncle Benito." Al Simon looked disappointed with that name. Damien sat quietly fighting back his emotions when he saw his family being led away. He wanted to say something but Oscar gave him a look that literally shut him up.

The eldest of the two girls could sense something amiss, like her mother's female intuition kicked in, "Dad?" She said. "Are you alright?"

"Yes my love." Damien said, struggling. "Follow your mother and make some breakfast alright. Daddy is just going to have a little chat with some friends over here. Alright?"

Oscar maintained his stony gaze on Damien. Damien needed to pull himself together, last thing Oscar and his men need right now is a complete nervous breakdown from Damien.

"You need to relax." Oscar spoke quietly. "I can't have you making a scene in front of your girls. We don't want to gag them and tie them up, but we will if you leave us with no choice."

"I understand, I should probably get dressed for work." Damien said. "This has to look like another normal day for me."

"Good. Very good. Uncle Benito will escort you upstairs to get your work uniform." Oscar said looking at Al Simon.

"You bring your work uniform here and change in front of us. Now get going." Damien stood up and dragged himself upstairs followed by Al Simon again. After a few minutes both men return with Damien's work cloths. Oscar frowned after seeing Al Simon also holding a black leather jacket and long jean trousers in hand.

Oscar shook his head and instructed Damien to get dressed. Damien did as instructed and got dressed in front of the gang. Al Simon did the same, Oscar was slightly annoyed but couldn't care less. Al Simon was being himself, there was nothing Oscar or anyone could do about it.

"It's almost seven." Oscar announced. "Make the call Damien. Call Maria Bonge and tell her that you are on your way to pick her up?"

"But, that's uncharacteristic of me," Damien said. "Her husband drops her off at work every morning."

Oscar moved closer and raised his gun, "I really don't care about that," said Oscar. "You do exactly as I say and you do it right. You make that call and make it right. Don't test me."

Damien reluctantly produced his mobile phone, slid through his contacts and pressed Maria Bonge's number. He pressed his phone against his ear with a shaky right hand and waited for the call to be answered.

"Hello?" a female's voice answered after the fourth ring.

"Maria, a very good morning to you."

"Morning Damien," her voice was rigid, mechanical. "What's up?"

"I'm going to drive up to your residence now and pick you up. There is something we have to discuss." Damien could barely focus. His mind was racing.

"Yeah, sure." Maria sounded slightly sceptical. "You are the boss."

"I appreciate that. I'll see you in the next ten to fifteen minutes."

"Okay." Damien ended the call. He gazed through the window. The first hint of dawn was shifting through the birch trees in his backyard, but the view looked somehow different this morning. An odd combination of fear and exhilaration settled over him.

Oscar moved forward. "Very good Damien," said Oscar, before switching his attention to his men.

"Alright listen up. The play commences this very hour. Don't get yourself attached to anything you are not willing to walk out from if you spot the heat around the corner. He who is without sin stays with the wife and kids. The rest . . . move out."

Chapter 35

Damian's tinted V8 eased away from Simbu Coffee, moving westward towards Wara Simbu Bridge. Familiar faces on the sidewalk strained to see through the tinted rear window, hoping to catch a glimpse of Damian.

I'm having a bad day friends, Damian thought, feeling miserable. No other car could offer him what he needed today – the guarantee of privacy. Total privacy.

A V8 in this country enjoyed a kind of unspoken immunity. Police officers were never certain what power broker they might mistakenly pull over in a V8, and so most simply chose not to take the chance.

But, in a small town like Kundiawa, Damian's V8 stole the show every time he drove through the small crowded town. A sea of eyes would turn his way to admire the beauty of this magnificent beast. Damian had always enjoyed the feeling of power he got from driving this massive car whenever he travelled on long journeys to the Eastern or the Western Highlands.

But today he felt powerless sitting inside his V8. As the V8 left Wara Simbu and ascended up Prenoroqua Hill, Damien could feel himself moving closer to Maria, pushed onward by an unfortunate fate. I am being forced to do something terrible, Lord forgive me.....my family's life depends on me right now.

Whether it was an inside job or not, the consequences of his action was certainly the last thing on Damian's mind. All he wanted right now is to get this over with real quick so he could see his pregnant wife and two daughters again. But, one thing Damian couldn't dismiss easily was the fact that the gang couldn't have picked a better time to rob Kundiawa Bank.

As bad as it was already, Oscar moved closer and whispered into Damian's left ear, "I want you to have this in mind that what you are doing right now is for your family. Believe me when I say that the last thing we want to do is hurt them. Don't give us an excuse to do it, because we will, in ways you cannot imagine. Be mindful of that," Oscar said.

"Don't stall. Maria needs to be inside the car before she realises what is going on, not outside. Understand?" Damian nodded vigorously, fighting to swallow the lump in his neck.

Oscar patted Damian's shoulder approvingly, "Good man. Relax and get on with the program. It will all be over shortly." It will all be over shortly.....the words echoed, that was precisely what Damian wanted above anything else in the world.

As the V8 made its final steady climb up past the Mobil fuel service station, and the Chimbu Premiers Inn, the bustling town came into view in all its usual routine; people as busy as ever as bees, buying and selling, working, arguing, fighting, unaware of the real trouble that was transported inside the tinted V8.

A sea of admiration and envious stares followed the V8 as usual as it came past the raucous Yuwai Market. A young male street vendor who was in his early twenties couldn't help but stare, "When will I ever own a car like that?" He said, hopelessly. "I will probably grow old and die wishing."

An elderly woman who stood beside the young man looked over with disgust, "That's why I told you to stay in school," she said, angrily. "Nothing was impossible. Now it's impossible."

The young man didn't speak. The elderly woman lit up her brus, shouldered a massive bilum bag of kaukau, dragged her small piglet by the leash, and walked off while mumbling sometime about money being wasted on school fees.

The V8 swerved right, passed the post office and the Kondom Agaundo Building, and the Chimbu Provincial Government headquarters. Leaving behind a cluster of supermarkets, department stores and kaibars in a rectangular shape that comprised the town, hence the name 'four corner town'.

Before 1934, the Kundiawa town area was a fighting zone for the Kamaneku and Endugla tribes and their allies. The Ega area where the school and mission headquarters is situated today was owned by the Kamaneku tribe. The Premier Hill area that Damien is driving towards is now known as Tema and the Malaria area but then was owned by the Endugla tribe.

A meeting between a German Lutheran missionary named Reverent William Bergmann, and a Kamaneku tribal chief named Bongere under very unlikely circumstances had paved the way for peace, and had set the foundation for what is now Kundiawa Town. By 1953, the Highlands Highway was built through the Chimbu-Wahgi post from Goroka.

This post, later named Kundiawa, became the capital of Chimbu in July 1966 when the area was declared a district of its own from Eastern Highlands. Kundiawa had since grown to be an important commercial and government centre for the Central highlands.

Inside the V8 now, heading towards the Premier Hill, everyone was silent, yet the intensity could be felt. The fear that now gripped Damian was a fear far greater than that of his own death. He felt his whole universe hung in the balance as the V8 descended down towards Wara Market.

Chapter 36

Less than a kilometre up the Premier Hill, Maria was just walking out of the gate when the shrill sound of her mobile phone cut the air. She pulled her phone from her bilum. Uncertain, she answered. "Hello?" The voice that spoke was eerie, a troubled whisper.

"Maria, are you outside the gate?" Maria felt uneasy. "Yeah, I'm standing outside now. Damien is everything alright?" She demanded, her words came out with a clear trace of concern. Everything Damien was doing today according to Maria had been amiss in every sense of the word.

"Everything is fine," Damian answered. "I'm turning into your street now."

"Damian why do I get the feeling you are not telling me something?" Maria said, suspiciously. "Are you sure everything is fine? You know I hate surprises." She heard a quick intake of breath over the phone and could feel Damian's annoyance.

"I just need to run a few things by you before we commence the day," Damian said. "Don't beat yourself up."

"If you say so. But like I said - I don't like surprises." You have no idea. Oscar gripped Damian's left shoulder and signalled him to end the call.

Maria opened her mouth to say something but the call was ended. Maria shook her head in disbelief and stared at her mobile phone. She raised her head again and saw the V8 curving its way around the bend, heading towards her. As the V8 drew closer, Maria quickly glanced at her mobile phone for the time: 07:15 AM Maria heaved a deep sigh. This had better be good, I didn't even finish my damn coffee, she thought.

The maroon, sleek V8 rolled to a stop beside Maria, and the driver's tinted window lowered silently. Maria poked her head around and forced a nervous smile. "Morning, Damian."

"Morning. Come in," said Damien, trying to force a smile. "Come to the front seat."

Maria gave a polite nod and walked around in front of the vehicle. She couldn't see through the tinted glass there were other people seated in the back seats. The minute she hopped inside and closed her door shut Damien started driving out. Maria realised that there was a dozen men cramped up in the back seats.

"Oh, I didn't know you brought company," Maria turned to look at them, in a professional tone. "Good morning all of you."

"Good morning sister," said Oscar, "We are coffee farmers from Karamui, our friend here said to assist us with opening an account for our association. Most of us are village folks, we don't bank our money. We usually keep money under our pillows, but you know…..we realise it's risky so we brought all our money here to bank. We are told you can be of assistance."

Maria stared at Damien. "Oh, yeah sure I can help you with that," said Maria. "It's not just you, many rural farmers around the country have the same issue. We try as much as we can to educate our rural farmers on financial literacy. It's good to bank your money."

"I understand, that's why I encourage the others to join me," said Oscar. "Last week my uncle's house accidentally got burnt to the ground with his three hundred thousand kina hard earned money hidden inside his suitcase. Everything burnt to ashes."

Maria shook her head, "That's why it is much safer to bank your money. I am so sorry for your uncle."

"Don't mention it, it's heart breaking," Oscar said, lying through his teeth. Al Simon quickly looked at Oscar convinced Oscar was actually telling a true story. Maria looked back.

"It looks like you farmers in Karamui have serious cash on hand….. all our money in Kundiawa must be locked up there. How much money are you trying to bank today?"

"Three point five million," Oscar said, plainly. Maria practically turned to look at Oscar, "I beg your pardon?" said Maria, surprised, "Did you just say three point five million?"

Oscar pulled out his gun. "That's exactly what I said, actually, you have that money, now you are going to bring me to it. Give me your key and the other combination to the vault. Don't test me."

Maria was shell shocked; it took her a few moments to digest the fact that she and Damien were being held up. The incredulous look of utter betrayal in Maria's eyes bore into Damian's skull excruciatingly.

"They have my family, I had no choice," said Damien, pleading, "There is nothing I can do. Please forgive me Maria."

Chapter 37

Susan was feeling ill that morning, she threw up all the beans and rice she had consumed the previous night. She sat beneath the bridge, drained. Normally she would slumber through the day but today was different.

She could sense something sinister hanging in the atmosphere that morning, and a strange fear churned deep in her gut. Susan wasn't aware Martha was standing behind her observing. Martha remained dead quiet.

Susan gradually could sense a human presence nearby. She swung around, "What the are you doing there?" Susan said, dreading the response. "Why didn't you tell me you were standing there?"

Martha maintained her gaze without uttering a word. Susan immediately got on her feet, "You are crazy. Stay away from me." Susan said as she tried walking past Martha, "You need help, go see a professional."

"Eventually it's going to show," Martha said in an amused tone. "You can't hide from it."

Susan stopped dead. "What are you talking about Martha?"

"The thing that is developing inside you."

"What the hell are you talking about?"

Martha studied Susan's face carefully, You don't know it yet - do you?"

"Know what? What are you talking about?"

"Susan - you are pregnant. It's written all over you."

Susan opened her mouth but not a single word materialised. She was stumped.

"Thomas is sterile, he can't produce kids, so I'm guessing - is it the guy from last night that started the fight?" Martha asked, candidly.

"I-I th-thats impossible" Susan said, tongue tied. She was struggling to speak, she could barely put two sentences together under Martha's stone cold regard.

"Nothing is impossible dear. It's him, isn't it?" Martha prodded.

Susan saw that Martha was already running her eyes all over her. Martha didn't look as disappointed as she should. After all, she's Thomas's sister.

"Martha it's not him," Susan said, barely fighting back the tears. "Please I beg you -"

"Listen dear. It's better that way," Martha cuts in, consolingly. "Thomas can't give you a child. You should keep it. To have children is your right, you can't be denied that - don't worry dear I won't tell a soul."

A powerful surge of emotions drove Susan towards Martha, she couldn't help but embrace Martha, "Thank you so much," Susan said, sobbing. "You are the only person who can help me now, I don't know what I am going to do. God bless you, Martha."

Martha shrouded her bony arms around Susan reluctantly, "It's alright dear," Martha whispered. "It's dry season, there is plenty of sunshine to go around. I will help you protect this child."

"What am I going to do?"

"You need to go back to your people. Listen to me," Martha held Susan's trembling hands. "I will give you some money for bus fare. No one will notice you sneaking out. If Thomas asks me, I will tell him nothing. By the end of the day I will make sure you are long gone."

"I - I don't know how to thank you Martha."

Martha smiled, "You can thank me once you are home free dear," said Martha. "Now. I want you to wait for me right here while I run to the house and get the money for your bus fare. Can you do that?"

"Yes."

"Good." Said Martha as she turned to leave.

"Wait," Susan said. "While you are at it can you fetch my bilum? It should be at the kitchen table, I can't leave that bilum, it was a gift from my grandmother."

Martha nodded understandingly, "Of course dear." Susan thanked Martha and watched as Martha walked off and went out of sight.

Susan couldn't stop her hands from shaking. She paced around aimlessly while her mind travelled to every worst possible scenario. By tradition Susan was now no longer a part of Thomas's family. Her womb carried another man's brood. It was a dangerous situation. In a way, she was behind enemy line.

Susan felt at that moment that she did not belong. She felt nature's scorn of violating a sacred tabu all around in the atmosphere. Wara Simbu suddenly seemed like a foreign hostile land. The chills deepened with each passing moment. Susan couldn't bare standing around any longer, she needed to go.

Susan abandoned her spot and traced after Martha regardless of what Martha had instructed. When Susan arrived near the house, she stood shrouded in the patch of bananas and scanned the area for Thomas. There was no one there. She kept looking around as she walked towards the house and briskly glided inside.

She went straight to the kitchen and saw that her bilum was still there, exactly the way she had left it. She snatched her bilum and was about to head outside again when the sudden realisation charged in, "Martha never leaves her money at home," Susan gasped.

At that moment she could hear the frantic muffle of Martha and Thomas approaching somewhere outside the house.

A chill surged through her whole being. Susan dashed inside her room and crawled under the bed. She could feel her heart in her windpipe.

"I'm going to murder that bitch I swear to God. Where is she?" Thomas said with raw determination as he walked past the house to look for Susan.

Martha followed close by, "I told her to wait for me under the bridge." Said Martha. "She doesn't know I went to get you; boy I'm really going to enjoy this."

From underneath the bed Susan could hear other people also following them. Susan held her breath. She was trapped. There was no way she could escape without being seen.

Chapter 38

Thomas along with Martha and at least twenty fervent locals arrived underneath the bridge at the spot where Martha had left Susan. Thomas turned to Martha, "Well, where is she?"

"I swear I left her standing right here." Said Martha. "She should be around here somewhere – "

"Where! Find her!" Thomas roared.

The crowd broke up and searched the riverside. Martha took another road up to the main highway just in case Susan went up there. She asked the vendors but no one saw Susan.

Thomas went downstream and searched the river banks. No sign of Susan anywhere. Martha returned from the roadside to join the search party. She knew Susan couldn't have gone anywhere, she's hiding somewhere, Martha thought, but where?

Martha came towards Thomas's house and walked past, then a thought materialised in her head and she stopped dead in her tracks. She slowly turned back, what if she's hiding inside the house? There was no one around there. The search party was conducted on the riverside. Martha was all alone there; an eerie silence dominated the atmosphere.

Martha slowly approached the house. She could feel deep in her guts that Susan was inside the house. Martha approached cautiously trying not to sound the alarm. The house door was open slightly, Martha slowly let herself in. She took the first step inside and looked around, before she took her second step she felt the back of her skull crushed in and she blacked out in an instant!

Susan stepped away and looked down at Martha who was lying unconscious on the floor. She held in her shaky hands the hard wood which she used to strike Martha. For a moment there, Susan wasn't sure if Martha was dead or alive, she looked closer and saw with relief that Martha was still breathing.

Susan peeked outside before stepping out and closing the door behind her leaving unconscious Martha laying on the floor. There was no one around who could have seen her, she quickly walked towards the coffee garden and disappeared.

Along the riverside Thomas was further away from the rest of the search party. He was contemplating the pain he will inflict on Susan when he gets his hands on her. Thomas conjured up all manner of ugly scenarios that are despicable in every sense of the word. God forbid. Thomas came to stop when he reached the threshold between the shale slates and the river, the only way to continue was to get inside the river and swim.

Thomas looked around, he let his eyes wonder further up "Lonely Mountain", memories of his previous life up in that mountain came back, reminding him of what had transpired many years ago under similar circumstances, in another life he thought, a life long forgotten.

As Thomas kept looking at the Mountain his eyes were drawn to a figure further downstream that was heading towards the road that went up Lonely Mountain. Thomas had to squint because of his poor eyesight, "It's her," Thomas said to himself. "Where are you going?"

Thomas could see Susan who was now heading up the road to Lonely Mountain, Thomas jumped inside the river without contemplating anything, swimming downstream, he was driven only by rage.

Chapter 39

Damien Tupa's pregnant wife Anna and her two daughters sat at the corner, (next to the fireplace) huddled together. Ialasam kept his eyes fixated on them. He wondered what it feels like to have a family, a family like Damian Tupa's family. Ialasam will never understand the happiness people get just being around family, though at times Ialasam secretly wished he could one day experience it but the whole idea always looked distant.

Things would have been a whole lot different if only the world around him could shed some light at the darkest corner of the house where that defenceless little boy sits alone and patiently waits for the scraps that fall from his own family's dinner table.

His stomach rumbles, yet his will is tougher than that of any man. He had disciplined himself never to express any sign of hunger as if it was a crime. He labours without food for hours until his small body cannot take the torture anymore and he would collapse, only then the world around him would recognise he needed something to eat.

Even the family's dog was better off than him. In the darkest corner of the house each night the little boy would sit alone, seeking refuge behind the shadow of his grandmother, the only person in the whole universe who truly understood him. But his grandmother had no power over the brutal dominion of the little boy's uncle. The little boy's name was only called when he bares the brunt of a cruel joke, his grandmother would simply tell him to ignore them. His name is only called when something goes missing; he would brave his uncle's belt with quiet whimpers and sit alone, his grandmother was always there to comfort him as he shrinks even smaller and sobs quietly in his dark corner till he falls asleep with dry tears on his cheeks.

His feelings meant nothing. Each and every night he sits where he belongs, in the corner, and watched their laughter and joyful faces, not a single soul in the room understood the hell that was brewing inside his gut.

For years he had been unjustly treated, he knew not what love was, only that of his grandmother. He had worked so hard to be accepted only to be treated with hate and disgust. The abuse had become chronic, and it seem the little boy's uncle's hidden motive was to kill the little boy, slowly, painfully.

The little boy's grandmother could no longer bear the pain; she could not stand helpless and watch while an innocent child was being tortured to death. Driven by raw grief she leapt off the cliff and killed herself.

The fire of hope dimmed in the little boy's heart. His only sanctuary in this cruel world no longer existed, and help was never coming. He was on his own....now more than ever, vulnerable.

A week after his grandmother was buried, the little boy gave in to his fate, he slowly walked to the cliff side which his grandmother had taken her own life and contemplated how the drop would end his.

He closed his eyes, hoping that death would be painless and quick. Before he launched himself down the misty chasm, a dark shadow loomed behind, came out of nowhere. The hands that grabbed at his shoulders felt as if they were infused with the power of the devil himself.

The man roared in his ear. NO!! The boy spun and struggled to free himself. Their eyes met. He was staring dead into the eyes of a complete stranger,

"You don't have to do this," the stranger said. "I understand what you are going through. I can help you, my son."

"You don't understand!" The little boy cried, struggling. "Nobody understands!"

The stranger held him close, tightly, hugging him, "Shh... sometimes we don't need anyone to understand us," the stranger said, whispering. "We only need to make them understand our pain."

The little boy felt as if the words were spoken inside his head. He had never felt such a powerful surge of conviction to trust someone before, "Who are you?" The little boy asked. "Why did you save me?"

The stranger explained that he was from the neighbouring village. "I saved you because you do not fear death. All that is human in you no longer exists - you are a perfect vessel my boy."

The little boy maintained his gaze trying to dispute the surreal connection with the stranger but he couldn't.

"You are a perfect specimen," the stranger said, beholding. "You do not belong in the light. You will dwell in the void...you are going to be the fuel that wrecks chaos. Tell me now, what do you desire?"

The little boy couldn't contain his fury, with a deep hatred he blurted out, "My uncle. I want him dead." He said, with loathing. "And everyone he loves."

"As you wish." The stranger replied with finality. Together they lured the little boy's uncle to the edge of the same cliff site, the little boy bursting out of nowhere plunged a knife into his uncle's back and shoves him off the cliff. His uncle screamed with horror, juddering desperately afloat briefly before descending down the misty chasm.

The final shriek echoed, and the horrified look on his uncle's face taunting inside the little boy's head. It took the little boy a while to register what he had just done. His uncle now lay at the bottom of the cliff; a lifeless body spread out on the limestone.

Dead.

The realisation charged in vigorously – he could feel the earth shifting beneath his feet. I killed him.

"You killed him." The stranger echoed his thoughts.

The little boy looked all around, frantically, searching everywhere if someone, anyone had noticed. But the location of the murder was on the blindside of the village – no one could have been around there to have witnessed.

"We have to hide the body," the stranger said. "Once the body rots, they will figure out where the corpse is. We will be long gone by then."

The boy wasn't listening. The surge of adrenaline guided him into a dreamlike state. Everything went blank and quiet; he felt his heart pounding like a desperate man on the door. A strange feeling of relief and satisfaction came over him.

Momentarily he held no regards to the consequences of what he had just done. His feeling – like a roller coaster at its slow steady ascent up the slope to its final descent; an endless drop of horror and fear that will soon befall him.

The boy still couldn't process what he had just done, but the stranger was there to encourage him, "this is what you have always wanted," the stranger said. "You should relish the moment. Don't fight it with fear, surrender yourself to the sensation."

In all the surge of emotions the boy drew his courage from the stranger who somehow managed to remain composed as ever. They quickly climbed down the cliff to where the corpse lay.

At first glance, the little boy couldn't stomach what he was looking at; bones sticking out of the skin and blood spraying from a cracked skull. He wasn't just looking at a dead body – he was looking at a badly disfigured human corpse. Slumped on the rocks, his dying uncle was still breathing, albeit barely, sucking in sputtering gasps. His eyes met the little boy's, and it was the same stony gaze only this time it was laced with utter disbelief.

The eyes looked even harder in death, the loathing and enmity rising to the surface. The boy watched as the stranger placed his hand over the dyeing man's quivering lips, "Before you die," the stranger whispered icily. "I want you to know that I am going to go back to your house tonight, and I am going to burn it down while your family's fast asleep."

The stranger then commanded the boy to stand over his uncle's head, take out his little prick and urinate right on the dyeing man's face. The boy reluctantly did. The boy looked down from his prick and glimpsed the intensity radiating from his uncle's eyes in the final seconds of his life from a blood and urine riddled face. His uncle, with tremulous effort, tried to say something as he was gargling piss and blood, but he died before he could make a sound.

Without a word they grabbed the corpse's foot both of them with both hands, and dragged it into a small opening in the earth well hidden beneath the reeds at the foot of the cliff. As the body was dragged deeper and deeper into the small tunnel, the boy discovered something else, something unlike anything before...a deep sensational feeling overcome him, a pleasure not induced by drugs, but the thrill of taking someone's life, someone who deserved to die, and that feeling shrouded his mind and consumed him.

The stranger looked over and smiled knowingly, "It's intoxicating, isn't it?" The stranger said, gleaming. "Unlike anything you have ever felt before in your life. It works better if you completely surrender to its power."

The boy did, and for seven hours they hid inside the cave with the corpse, savouring the scent of death until they could feel the midnight cold. Still pumped with adrenaline they quietly crept out of the cave back to the village and razed the hut where the woman and her two children were sound asleep inside.

He thought, for years this evil woman and her two demonic children have plagued on me, stood by and laughed at my suffering. Now I will have the last laugh at theirs. The boy watched the fire grow, he wanted to see it through, watch them burn and scream to their death, but he knew once the screaming starts the neighbours will respond.

In the hype of the moment the stranger stared at the boy square in the face, "you have to go now," the stranger said. "But I give you two options: firstly, if you run now without turning back, you will be on your own, I will no longer follow you. But, if you turn back for a second to have a glimpse at this burning house, I promise I will be with you forever."

"How does the second option work?" The boy asked. "What am I getting into?" "I will always be with you." The stranger said. "We will be united in spirit forever."

"What do you -" the boy stopped dead in horror, his jaw dropped, he couldn't fathom what he was seeing. The stranger suddenly seemed to be slowly disintegrating right before his eyes. HE IS VANISHING!

"I will dwell in you..." And the stranger vanished totally right before the boy's eyes. The boy gasped. The flames became relentless, gradually devouring the house. Before long he heard the first horrific scream of the woman coming from inside the burning hut, a chorus of dreadful cries following right after.

Screams of horror and agony, consumed by a mindless monster that knows no mercy, devouring all its victims. Still shaken the boy fled before the alarm was raised. He fought with the bushes until he came to the threshold between the village and the forest.

Before he moved any further, he paused. He knew if he turned back to have a glimpse, he would be making a pact with God knows what, because the stranger was no human.

In that defining moment he realised he needed the power from a different dimension if he wants to live. He turned his whole body and surrendered himself with totality to the entity. Something entered him, he could feel the sudden transformation. He looked forward with eyes that were no longer human and saw the flame lighting up the whole village, a wicked smile swept across his face before he fled into the ghastly forest, embracing his dark nature, and finding sanctuary in the devils embrace.

The screams of those inside the flame lingered inside his head, a choir from hell, a foul melody that fuelled his drive to run further away from the village as possible and never return, the beast in him rejoiced, he had accomplished his ultimate goal.

With the power and the direction of the beast inside he travelled through the forest from Chimbu to the Eastern Highlands. When he arrived in Goroka Town, he discarded his real identity and promised never to resurrect his old demoralised self, he was born again, in fire and blood, he called himself Ialasam, a name which creates the illusion of innocence but reflects his true nature when reflected in a mirror: IALASAM | MASALAI.

Hiding in plain sight. Moving like a snake under the cover of darkness to satisfy the growing needs of the beast within.

A dark cloud hovered above wherever Ialasam went. Bringing destruction and chaos without being caught. He was invincible. Over the years as he grew older his insatiable desire to commit crime knew no boundaries. He no longer commits crime to survive as he normally did, he was in for the thrill of it.

Other criminals whom he was working with grew weary of his unconventional methods, they say: "he had no soul"...he was bad for business; they realised they needed to put an end to his life. They secretly planned to have him killed, beheaded, chopped to pieces and buried...but he was there that night, hiding in the shadows, listening to each and every word that came out of their mouths.

He was a creature born out of darkness; there was no way anyone could have seen him. When they had dispersed, he came out of the darkness with a clever and cunning plan of his own.

For his evil plan to work he only needed to lure his crew with one last score, he knew they couldn't refuse the action. Their plans to have him killed would have to wait, because the score was a six men job. After the massive score had been successfully pulled off, he would lure the crew to a remote safe house for the breakup. He knew they couldn't say no to a convenient spot where they could easily have him killed.

He had them thinking that they were leading him into his grave, but it was 'he' who was leading them into their graves. That night at the remote safe-house only one man walked out alive with the loot.

The police arrived an hour later at the scene via an unanimous tip off, naturally the public assumed the police killed all of the criminals and blamed it on someone else just to hide the money.

Over a span of two years, he had cunningly lured in five of the most notorious gangsters in the Highlands to their demise and walked off with the scores. Each time the police would arrive a little too late and bare the full brunt of his actions.

No one knows he exists, those who do are never alive to tell. Now as he sits there looking at Damian Tupa's family, he came to the sudden realisation that not everyone who was responsible for the hell he endured as a child and the death of his grandmother were killed, one person still remains.

That person must also die.

The fire in the center danced inside Ialasam's lifeless dark eyes, a glimpse of a soul chained inside the dancing flame to the rhythm of the cries of horror that fuel his burning desire for terror.

Chapter 40

The V8 idled around the bank and parked right in front of the main entrance, a few meters away from the bank's tinted glass doors. It was a calculated move to conceal all that was about to go down; blocking the view of anyone outside the bank.

Damian sat behind the wheel motionless. He could feel his heart rate accelerate. He couldn't stomach what he was doing, he suddenly felt like a traitor. Lord please tell me this is just a bad dream – Damian felt Oscar's ferocious grip on his right shoulder, Oscar's voice transformed instantaneously to a raspy whisper, "keep the car engine running. Get out of the car. Walk to the entrance and go inside. Act normal. Maria is counting on you, not to mention your beloved wife and daughters."

It wasn't a request. Damian turned to lock one last gaze with Maria before letting himself out of the car. He fought hard to maintain composer as he paced towards the bank's entrance.

The tentative security guard outside smiled inquisitively. Damian nodded reluctantly. He wasn't sure how to react. How could the guard, let alone anyone guess? Who would have bothered to think that there was something amiss about Damian's routine that morning. Why would they?

Kundiawa Bank has never been robbed before. The guard kept his undeterred smile as he held out his right hand to give Damian a handshake as always. "Good mor – "

Bursting out of thin air, with extraordinary violence, Damian is slammed against the guard as if by a savage rugby player.

Dei Kembol, who is now masked and armed shoved Damian against the guard inside the bank with brute force. He collided with the guard before the guard had the chance to greet him, their combine weight whacked the door open as they crashed on the tiles inside the bank.

The early morning sun rays poured in onto the white tiles that radiated the rays all around the Bank's interior.

It all happened under a second, the two security guards inside the bank didn't have time to complete a blink before Dei Kembol materialised with his gun aimed at them, "stay where you are! Don't move or breathe unless I tell you to!"

The two guards froze. Three more armed, masked men moved past them shouting, "Take your mobile phones out and raise them with both your hands! Do it now!"

The stunned employees were pushed back and forced to lay flat on the floor.

Al Simon reached over the counter and grabbed a teller, lapelled and yanked him over the counter top and throw him across the floor, he then jumped over the counter and goes after the two female employees in the back.

Oscar quickly glanced up at the majestic Calarco Clock which had always been a spectacle when customers enter the lobby. But today, the Calarco's beauty stood idle - it's function was needed for the event that could well determine the future of the bank which it served.

"Seven thirty men!" Oscar announced. "Let's make this in two minutes."

Two minutes indeed. Oscar had to table the two minutes rule; get in, get the cash, and get out. Do it under two minutes. If it takes longer than two minutes, add it to your 'To Do List' rather than task switching from whatever you are currently doing.

Dei Kembol pulls the door shut, walks back and yanked Damien up from the floor, and shoved him forward, "Let's go. The volt. Now."

Jim Rento continued zip tying the bank employees with their hands behind their back face first on the tiled floor. The gang knew that they can count on compliant victims. Most banks consistent with police advice direct employees to comply quickly with robbers demands.

Oscar stood over the people on the floor. "Listen up! This bank is being held up!" Oscar announced.

"We do not want to hurt anyone! We are only here for the money! If you cooperate with us you will walk out of here unharmed, you have my word!" Oscar strode to his left, "Keep your heads down with your hands behind your back!"

Oscar than jumped over the counter to get a better vantage point, "Do not try to be a hero! Now is not the time! The money you earn is not enough to risk it, if you try anything stupid – " Oscar noticed something.

He jumped down the counter, and strode over towards an elderly male staff member who was still sitting behind his desk. When the staff member saw Oscar approaching, he quickly removed his hand which was inches away from the alarm button.

Oscar came forward and slams a punch into the old timer's face in calculated contrast to his friendliness. It was an object lesson to the rest of the employees of the result of disobeying.

The old timer flipped backwards over his chair and groaned.

Oscar dragged the old timer out, mauled him to the floor, and zip tied his hands behind his back all too tightly.

Dei Kembol continues shoving Damien forward, "The volt. Let's go."

Oscar followed them. They arrive in front of the massive chrome vault. Oscar inserted the vault key and motioned Damien for the combination. Damien reached for the big dial with a trembling hand, before he could start rotating Kembol pressed the gun against his head.

"How many attempts before a duress delay?" Kembol asked. " Th-three." "You don't want us here forever, trust me."

Damien reached for the dial again and begin working the numbers. After the third turn, there was a click. Oscar spun the wheel and the vault door opened. The powerful, intaglio scent of money wafted out of the steel inner sanctum. For an instant Oscar and Kembol stood paralysed with their eyes wide open. The insider was dead on; stash after stash of cash in all assorted colours lined the metal shelves inside the vault like books on a book shelve.

Dei Kembol gasped, "please tell me this is not a dream," he whispered, enchantingly.

Oscar ignored him and quickly walked inside the vault, and frantically started raking the stash of money from the shelves into the first bag. He didn't realise that he was shaking. The money continuously poured into the bag like a long slurp of honey pouring into a cup.

Dei Kembol thought it was the most beautiful thing he had ever seen. He knocks out Damien cold and zip ties him face first and waltzed into the vault to assist Oscar. He opens the Hefty Garbage bag disembowelled, spills money.

Oscar loads into three Hefty bags Kembol holds open. They wiped the safe clean from hundreds, fifties and twenties.

Once the first bag was full Oscar zipped it up, slid it out, and immediately worked on getting the second bag filled. At the lobby Jim Rento and Al Simon stood guard, watching the bank staff who were lying flat on their bellies, face first on the floor.

Mike Rento glanced up at the massive Calarco Clock, "seven thirty five!" Mike announced, "let's go! Let's go!"

Oscar materialised tossing one money bag on his shoulder like a sailor's duffle bag, his machine gun in front and walks to the lobby passing everyone. Dei Kembol follows right behind with three more bags sliding two across the floor towards Mike and Al Simon.

Inside the V8 paranoia churned deep in Jim Rento's gut with each passing second. He was sitting in the driver's seat. The time seem to be moving in slow motion. He started to become restless and agitated in his seat. He could see a group of people supposedly customers eagerly congregating outside the bank's premises, behind the steel gate waiting for the bank to open. The bank was supposed to be opened fifteen minutes ago.

Maria sat motionless, but she could easily sense the tension in Jim Rento's movement; he was shifting around restless in the leather seat, and sighing deeply for no other obvious reason than to get this robbery over with really quickly. Maria knew dead well that now was not the best of times to try anything stupid, because out of fear and panic Jim Rento could easily kill her without a blink.

A scared and cornered wild animal can be extremely lethal.

As Jim Rento continued to watch the crowd outside the bank's gate his heart rate accelerated when he saw a sky blue police land cruiser idling in front of the small crowd, "oh shit... this isn't happening," said Jim.

Maria saw Jim Rento switching off the safety and held his AK47 abreast. He was ready for World War 3. Maria gulped. If anything happens right now she would be right in the middle of a crossfire. The thought alone made her sick to the pit of her stomach. Maria couldn't help it anymore, she was suddenly sobbing quietly, "p-please let me go...y-you don't need me anymore," pleaded Maria.

"Shh...I need you now more than ever," Jim said. Maria (morbidly) thought it sounding almost romantic, but there was not a glint of emotion registered on Jim Rento's face. Jim was composed. Very composed.

It took Maria a while to realise what exactly Jim Rento intends to do with her. Her heart skipped a beat. He's going to use me as a shield! Maria begins sobbing uncontrollably, "p-please I have two kids," Maria said, painfully. "You don't have to do this. I'm begging you, please." Maria kept looking around, her eyes glistening with tears, for a moment there she thought that Jim seemed almost convinced. But then she realised that he wasn't even paying attention.

Maria suddenly felt meagre, like a complaining child. Her words fell on deaf ears. Jim was no longer with her, grave matters seemed to bombard his thoughts so as not to heed the plea of a woman. The enormity and the magnitude of the situation compelled a total eclipse of human emotion from Jim.

Outside the bank's gate now, Jim could see three police men hopping out of their vehicle. One of them walked up to the gate and seemed to be shouting. Jim couldn't hear anything over the sound of Maria sobbing inside the airtight V8.

The officer who was complaining outside the gate was pointing to his watch indicating his disappointment. They were all harmless, disgruntled customers unaware of anything. No one could see anything happening from the driver's side of the V8.

The bank's entrance to the main lobby was concealed. The massive vehicle completely blocked that line of sight.

Oscar now exited the bank via the side door and moved quickly towards the parked getaway V8, his facemask off, his AK47 low, concealed. Mike Rento and Al Simon followed.

Oscar opened the V8's door and dumped the bag in the back seat, Jim Rento swings around and takes a good look at the tight hefty bag.

"Oh man," said Jim, "we have company outside the fence, but they don't know anything yet."

Oscar glanced through the tinted glass and saw two Police Officers smoking cigarettes and talking with people outside the bank's fence. Mike Rento and Al Simon arrived there and tossed their bags in the back seat, they also saw what Oscar saw, "that's not good," said Oscar, "where's Kembol?"

Al Simon swings around, "he's right behind," said Simon, "where is he?" Jim Rento was now suddenly calm and alert. All three men got inside the car on one side and pulled the car door shut. Jim idles the engine while braking with his left foot. The atmosphere inside the car intensifies.

Al Simon's patience ran out, "where's the Western Highlander?" said Al Simon, edgy, "don't tell me he went back."

Going back was precisely what Dei Kembol did. Inside the bank Dei Kembol went back into the vault to collect the marked bills. Kembol frantically tries to fill up two hefty bags at the same time, Kembol was panting, blindly consumed by greed, there was no way in the world he would walk out without taking everything. He wanted it all.

The two guards at the lobby crouched towards the vault and Dei Kembol. They gravely underestimated Dei Kembol, their shadows betrayed them. Kembol was already on his feet aiming his AK47 directly at them when the first guard reared his head. The gun roared inside the chrome vault. The guard fall backwards. He was gone.

Kembol ran out and shot the second guard on the back. Someone at the lobby pressed the alarm button.

The V8's engine screams as it peals out directly towards the gate. In a matter of seconds all hell broke loose!

Dei Kembol was on his own.

Chapter 41

About the same time Oscar and his gang started walking out of the Kundiawa Bank, the Kundiawa Police Officials were handling what seemed like another normal day at their headquarters.

The Provincial Police Commander Kombri Gigma sat down comfortably in his chair outside his office, on the lawn with a reporter. Both the PPC and the reporter had just attended a swearing-in ceremony for new officers. The reporter was asking about an incident that occurred in Kerewagi were an innocent bystander was accidently shot during a speedy car chase.

"Ah, look here son," said Kombri, leaning forward, "it is easy to criticise the tactics of my officers. Like most things in this complicated world of ours, nothing is ever simple. Every police event is fluid. However, many other extenuating factors played a critical role in this tragic event."

"Such as?"

"Well, this department is in the midst of a bankruptcy that has robbed us of many veteran officers. Some of those officers were replaced with rookies straight out of the college." Kombri paused to let that sink in.

"This basically means we are working within our means; we might not be as efficient as we should. Such accidents are prone to happen. I sincerely apologise to the victim who just happened to be at the wrong place at the wrong time."

The reporter nodded and quickly took down notes. The reporter was well aware of the PPC's frankness; he had been interviewing Kombri for the last three years to understand the kind of man he was dealing with. Kombri doesn't filter what he says. His interviews are usually off the record types. The reporter knows he must filter his interview and make Kombri look presentable in the papers.

Kombri spoke again as the reporter was scribbling notes into his notebook, "in spite of some of our flaws and due to situations beyond our control – we still manage to get the job done. Criminals are arrested and locked-up, we are still producing results to the best of our ability."

"In light of that," the reporter said, clearing his throat, "has there been any developments in relations to the seven highway robberies in Talis? We understand the crimes are committed in similar fashion."

Kombri felt meagre all over sudden. "Well, this kind of criminal acts are known as 'repeat victimisations. These repeat robberies occur because of the easy escape route that remains unchanged. But I'm going to be frank here," Kombri sighed heavily. "We now have a fair idea who is behind all these highway robberies. The foggy bandits as you so eloquently describe them will eventually be caught. I guarantee you we will still catch up with them. We are now aware of their pattern and how they move. The next time they decide to strike we will be ready – "

Before Kombri could complete his sentence, the rapid discharge of a machine gun somewhere near on the southern side of Kundiawa Town silenced him. Both men exchanged baffling looks.

Kombri's first thought was the police dispersing a crowd with warning shots. But in less than two seconds after the first shots could be heard, a line of shots proceeded right after.

The sound of gunshots reverberated all around the corridor of 500-meter tall limestone outcrop stretching east to west and in the north, with enough power to startle the bustling town with its estimated population of over 15,000 people.

It came from the weapon whose sound was so recognisable. A gunfight? Kombri thought.

Kombri jerked upright from his chair. Kombri looked around, he couldn't believe there was a war going on few blocks away from his office.

Kombri roared, "What's going on!" No one responded. All the officers in sight looked completely lost, "What the hell is going on!" Kombri screamed with rage.

The reporter shivered and excused himself. The interview was over anyway.

Outside the police station's corrugated fence Kombri could see people screaming and shouting all over the town. Kundiawa Town had exploded into chaos; men, women and children screamed with horror and ducked for cover everywhere. It was as if the Pandora box had been opened and all manner of foul creatures had plagued the town.

Amidst the pandemonium someone screamed from his lungs, "the Kundiawa bank's being robbed!"

"Men! Guard all the business houses for looters! Now!" Kombri roared one order and sped into the station to see operations deputy chief.

In the nearby holding cell, Raskols who were locked up inside the cell started rejoicing; clapping their hands, and joyfully singing, sarcastically, while the shocked stricken officers scrambled for rifles and vests, neither of which were given to individual officers; instead, they were given out on a first-come, first served basis. There was not enough for everyone.

Constable James Balkane threw away the steaming cup of Kongo Coffee he was about to have and bolted out of the gate. James shouldered his gun and took the frontline without any sense of self-preservation. He ran past every other officer, including the ones who had bullet proof vests. No one tried to stop him.

Chapter 42

"This is like new years Eve on steroids! Except, this one's in broad daylight!"

The daredevil driver said as he raced in and out of traffic at Prenorokwa Hill to get to the town. Nem riding shotgun.

Nem's blood coursed with raw fury. He was still trying to process the fact that these criminals had brought the war to his doorstep. The sound of cocked guns came one after another from the back adjacent seats of the Ten-Seater-Toyota Land Cruiser.

The four young, athletic police men, with their buzz cuts were composed and ready, like soldiers prepared for combat. Nem shifted in his seat and cocked his gun, "They come to my town. Rob my bank. And made a fool out of me.....I promise you, before the sun sets today, I will bathe in their blood." Nem said, with determination.

The daredevil driver quickly glanced over; Nem looked terrifying. The driver felt a chill up his spine. He spoke no more. Nem would often refer to Kundiawa Town as 'his town'. Being an Endugla man he saw everyone else as guests. Nem's people were the first in Chimbu to use guns in a tribal fight between the Nauro's in 1982, the fight developed into a civil war, Nem was just a teenager at that time when he charged into battle.

Over three decades later and he was charging into a different kind of battle in the very same place.

Reports of the bank robbery crackled out from all police radios. Every police officer within the Town radius leapt into action. The radio traffic made sure everyone involved understood the severity of the undertaking at hand.

Officers could be heard over the police radio stating their vehicles were taking rounds from the AK-47. In some cases, the sounds of bullets striking the vehicles could be heard.

Kundiawa Town instantly became off limits to the travelling public. All manner of locomotives from the Eastern Highlands were halted in Wara Simbu, and those from the Western Highlands were halted in Gon Hill.

Those who were already inside the town made quick detours and fled in all directions, some as far as Sigiwagi to the north west.

When the chaos was at its peak, Nem and his unit stormed the Town. Looters fled for their lives at the sight of Nem's car, like rats scrambling everywhere.

"Sonofabitch!" Nem turned to the driver, blood boiling. "They are already outside! We will take them inside the car! Run into them if you must!"

The driver complied without a response. He drove at the cruiser's top speed towards the TNA shopping mall, and then made a hard right, a perfect 90 degrees turn, and revved the engine past the post office.

It was there that they saw the maroon V8 struggling at the intersection. Police officers were everywhere; crouching behind their vehicles, hiding behind trees, some laying down on their bellies, some running, and others simply stood and fired and continued to fire shot after shots at the V8.

Those inside the V8 responded to the aggression equally.

Nem fastened his seat belt tightly, "Run into them!"

"A collision course?!" The driver said, not sure if he heard correctly.

"Hell yeah!" Nem roared.

The four young officers in the back back exchanged terrified looks and immediately gripped the edge of their seats. Bracing themselves for impact. There was no time to contemplate. We have no bloody seat belts here!

The driver was now dead certain Nem had lost it, nonetheless he reluctantly hit the accelerator, peeling out through the chaotic street. The suspects in the back of the V8 kept firing.

In that moment, the driver's mind wandered into darkness. He had just met with his life insurance guy the day before. It was a morbid thought, but in that defining moment he knew his family would be taken care of. At approximately forty metres before they came into collision with the V8, a torrent of bullets showered upon the cruiser, shattering the front headlights and the windscreen. Nem ducked beneath the dashboard, while the driver tried to zigzag while driving, trying to avoid the bullets, but the bullets struck out both front tyres of the vehicle.

In a dreamlike state the cruiser tilted and flipped in one motion, sliding on the driver's side across the road and came to halt on a power cable pole. Miraculously, no one was hurt.

Nem smashed the windscreen outward and emerged from the wreckage. He looked over and saw the V8 was no longer in sight. He went around to check on his men, they were all fine with bruises, "You guys alright?"

"We're good boss. They won't get far. They will run into the Kerowagi Mobile Squad if they are traveling the Gumuni road."

"I hope they bring one of them alive here so I can kill him myself –"

The sound of gunshots coming from the Airport side of the town stopped Nem from talking. Nem looked over and saw some officers running towards the Airport. One of the officers was saying, "They left one of their men behind!"

Without thinking, Nem ran after the officers towards the airport.

Chapter 43

"Jim!" Oscar screamed from the backseat of the commandeered V8.

For a moment everyone inside the vehicle held their breaths, they were all dead certain the machine which they rode in would crash into the main gate of the Kondom Agaundo Building, the SPG headquarters.

Maria kept her eyes tightly shut and gripped her seat belt. Her knuckles all white. The V8 made a full brake in the middle of the intersection. As the V8 careened to a stop less than fifty meters later, the gunfire kept on coming.

The gunfire roared as more than 600 shots were fired. In some cases, officers inexplicably opened fire with their colleagues standing in front of them. Some officers lay prone on the ground, at the same time, their colleagues standing above them fired off shot after shot.

From the right back seat window, Al Simon stuck out his AK-47 and sprayed 7.62-mm rounds, disabling a police vehicle that was heading directly towards them from the Post Office.

"Make left! Make left!" Oscar shouted frantically.

Jim Rento reversed the vehicle and made a hard left whilst Al Simon continued his shooting spree. Before they knew it, Jim Rento gunned the V8 down Kundiawa Main Market road.

The look of utter shock and confusion dominated the faces of every bystanders who now became the passing scenery.

The gang didn't plan for this. They were now only acting on their survival instincts, like wild animals set loose in a crowded market place. The V8 weaved through, almost getting trapped at another intersection at Wara Market where there were massive potholes.

Bystanders cried with rage and threw lime stones at the V8. Al Simon responded accordingly sending the angry mob scrambling for their lives.

"Turn left!" Oscar shouted again.

Jim Rento swerved into the Gumuni Road and gunned the vehicle up the small hill through a tree-lined neighbourhood. As they reached the top of the climb, the former Kundiawa General Hospital like an abandoned ship fell below them. Oscar looked east towards the town and saw three police land cruisers rolling down, it was like watching from an adjacent conveyer belt.

"Drive straight ahead!" Oscar ordered. "Drive like the world is coming to an end!"

"Oscar! Mirane will be barricaded for sure!" Jim Rento said. "You want us to go through the Police Barack?"

"We'll ditch the car anywhere if we run into trouble!" Oscar said with finality.

Jim obeyed his navigator, driving south towards Mirane. Inside the V8, the feeling was one of ecstasy laced with fear.

Bullet casings were everywhere from shooting out the back windows. The smell of gunpowder was overwhelming. As the vehicle curved its way down and around the pothole ridden Gumini Road towards Dogor, Jim Rento was unaware of the fact that Maria had already unbuckled her seat belt.

Maria knew there were no rules of engagement in such circumstances, everyone in the vehicle was marked for death and she along with them. She was helplessly caught in between a vicious fight between two blood enemies. She glanced over and noticed that her door was locked. She shifted her leg toward the door lock to see if the driver was paying attention. He was not. She knew the door would automatically lock itself. She nonchalantly unlocked the door and in one motion all she could remember was her door and the handle.

Maria launched herself at an intersection, cartwheeling across the limestone dirt road, from the V8 that was going 50 miles per hour. She blacked out. Jim Rento made a hard brake, "What the fu-" The opened door slammed shut!

"Go!"

Oscar shouted. Jim stepped on the accelerator again. He didn't stop to see if Maria was alright, the idea was to get the door shut all by itself by coming to an abrupt halt when the vehicle was in motion, because he sure as hell wasn't leaning over and waste time closing the door. They could hear the police sirens nearing.

"Brave woman!" Jim Rento said. "What was she thinking?!"

"Casualty of war," Oscar said, coldly. "When it rains everyone gets wet."

Al Simon stood on his right knee on the car seat, and turned around to see where Maria had landed through the shattered back windscreen. As he did so he noticed something else and let out a distraught groan, "No no no!"

Oscar immediately stood on his knees as well and turned. When Oscar saw what Al Simon was looking at, he knew their problems had just got worse.

"What is it?!" Jim Rento asked. Oscar and Al Simon exchanged sceptic looks. The V8 had already came around the bend at Dogor, Oscar knew it was the perfect spot for an ambush if the police in Mirane intended to do one.

"What the hell is it?!" Jim Rento shouted with rage.

Oscar was hesitant, "Mikes, Mikes is gone -"

Before Oscar could complete, he spotted armed men in blue uniforms moving inconspicuously amongst the roadside reeds all around the bend.

The vehicle slowed down, Jim Rento somehow no longer had the will to carry on. He lowered his head and started sobbing. The heat was around the corner, they were boxed in, any man who was not willing to walk out of an attachment in a split second is as good as dead.

In that moment Oscar realised that Jim Rento was not coming. Split second, thirty seconds, two minutes, an hour, or even eternity - Jim Rento could never walk away from his brother.

Al Simon swung his door opened, snatched a bag of cash, jumped out of the car and opened fire - all in rapid motion. Oscar followed suit. Before long the police vehicles in pursuit from Kundiawa materialised at a new distance up the road with sirens and headlights.

They were now cornered in all directions. There was no way out by car.

Chapter 44

The continuous terrifying sound of high-powered rifles corralled everyone back further and further into their shells.

Dei Kembol frantically ran east towards the airport. He was like a wild beast singled out from the herd by hungry lions.

He somehow managed to climbed over the airport's corrugated intertwined fence amidst the bullets heading his way, and made haste on the airport runway towards the end of the airstrip. If he made it down the gorge, the river and the forest was his element.

Only the brave would risk their lives coming after him that far.

He knew there was still a chance of getting out of his predicament alive, if only he could make it to the end of the airstrip.

The officers in pursuit realised what Dei Kembol intended to do. They all came to an abrupt halt after comprehending the risk involved in going after him in an open area, but another officer swiftly arrived, ran past them, and climbed over the barbed wired corrugated intertwined airport's fence with superb athleticism and scampered on the airport runway after Dei Kembol.

The officers stood speechless and looked at each other. The lone officer pursuing Dei Kembol clearly had more determination than all of them – this had to be personal. Einstein said, two things are infinite, the universe and human stupidity, the officers standing there at loss weren't sure about the first.

Into the misty Kundiawa Airport an energetic and determined Constable James Balkane ran, puffing, with sharp reflexes scanning the runway to catch a glimpse of Dei Kembol. This was his moment to shine, catching Dei Kembol could turn his whole career in the force around.

James's heart raced as he proceeded towards the end of the airstrip. James slowed down and held out his pump action. This time James held out the gun firmly with both hands, the gun pressed against his right shoulder, his index finger trembling on the trigger.

James realised he had run a great distance towards the end of the airstrip. The end of the airstrip was a no-go zone, and it felt somewhat distant from the town. The atmosphere there seemed strangely quiet, except the continuous sound of his heart beating.

James shook his head to dismiss the fear and continued looking around, occasionally turning sharply at the slightest unusual noise. The faint sound of a light aircraft somewhere above did little to remind James that he was right in the middle of the airport runway. His whole attention was diverted towards catching Dei Kembol, for all he cares the airport authority can call off all flights until he completed his mission.

James was driven by purpose, there was no time to explain as he so valiantly demonstrated earlier on in front of the officers he had left behind. James elusively recognised the unmistakable sound of the light aircraft hovering above, most likely belonging to a prominent local businessman.

The local pilots were notorious; some local pilots have had the distinction of flying so low that foliage and tree branches got stuck in their tail-wheels.

The sound of the aircraft engine above seemed to be getting louder, and then it decreased gradually as the plane drew away.

James didn't realise nor did he pay any attention to that, he was caught up in the hunt he couldn't afford paying attention to any other thing besides catching Dei Kembol. In an almost dreamlike state, James indefinably heard the sound of the light aircraft getting louder and louder by the second. He stood idle for a moment trying to work out why the light aircraft's sudden increasing sound should be his concern. The idea that he was on the runway hadn't settled in yet.

Before James came to his senses – the aeroplane appeared out of nowhere from the south exploding the mist metres away from him, James shrieked with horror and dived to his right seconds before the light engine airport propeller missed him by just inches!

The light flashed before James's eyes, a second later and he would have been sliced and run over. James cursed in agony upon landing on his elbow. He had scraped off a fair bit of skin. His blood dripped onto the airstrip tar like a blood offering, a blood offering in memory of the people who assembled in line seventy years ago hauling rocks from Wara Simbu to Kundiawa from dusk till dawn laying the foundation of the airstrip which James now set on.

James didn't realise that he had pissed himself.

Finally, it settled in with James that the plane only hovered above in the 'holding' procedure, the pilot couldn't have seen anything bellow because of the mist, compounded with the fact that there aren't any air traffic control (ATC) to actually guide, the local pilot just swoops the plane in as he does so out of routine – swooping the plane in after the brief holding.

Still on the ground gasping for air James's left eye caught the slight glimpse of someone standing on the southern end of the airstrip.

James abruptly got on his feet and came face to face with Dei Kembol who was aiming his gun directly at him. James felt the blood drain from his face. He stared in horror, unable to look away. James closed his eyes tightly, and all he could hear was a single shot, like thunder piercing the sky.

He shuddered. His heart throbbed. He felt no pain, yet all he could see now was darkness. James slowly opened his eyes and realised that he was still well alive, unharmed.

He looked over and saw Dei Kembol laying out dead on the airstrip runway. James looked to his right, on the far corner close to the airport fence Commander Nem stood with his gun in hand.

Nem had shot Kembol seconds before Kembol had the chance to pull his trigger.

Chapter 45

The bend at Dogor was covered in reeds and thorns, it was also used as an illegal waste disposal area….. an ugly place for a stroll. But the two men now fighting through the bushes held equal determination with no regards to the surroundings.

Their plight was one of life and death. They were no longer bank robbers…..they were now cop killers. Surrendering was no longer an option. Through eternal condemnation they took flight.

The gunshots echo from far above. Beseeching.

Oscar relied only on irregular sightings every now and then as Al Simon zig-zagged through the bushes. Bulldozing his way through the shrubs. Smelling the rotten vegetation. Huddling in the shadows of Erekolas.

With their heavy bags of cash swinging by their sides, they had dodged bullets, and run down a great distance from the roadside. With adrenaline coursing through their veins, Al Simon kept going down, frantically, all the while certain that Oscar was right behind him.

Bursting out of the bushes Al Simon suddenly came to an abrupt halt at the fringes of the clifftop. Gasping. He stood breathless as he stared down the unforgiving gorge. Eagles soared in large circles above.

Beyond the cliff, far below he could see the river junction; the junction served the Wara Simbu, which snaked its way down from the north and the Waghi River, which pushed its way east. At the Y-junction he saw the two different coloured rivers blend with ease as in unison they squeezed through the basalt rocks to the south east.

Oscar soon arrived beside him without warning, "we have to get down there fast," Oscar said, panting. "Once we hit the river, they will never catch us. Come on."

Without discussing it Oscar quickly walked to the edge of the cliff which was dominated my flowering mountain laurels. He was searching for a suitable spot to climb down. When he finally spotted one, he wasn't wasting time.

"Sai C'mon!" He said, as he quickly removed the heavy bag of money off from his shoulder and dumped it down the cliff, "weight's going to drag us down," he said. "We have to let go of the bags."

For a moment there Al Simon held his breath…..holding it, until he finally heard the thud of the money bag landing somewhere. Surprisingly the thud sounded close by. He rushed over and saw that the money bag had landed on a ledge about 60 feet down, wide enough to park a land cruiser.

Without hesitation Oscar swung his gun back, got on his knees, slid over the edge, and carefully lowered himself down; grabbing the shrubs and jutting rocks for steady descent, he had to control his footing firmly in the right direction, if he lost his footing it would be like falling from the top of a six-storey building, that is if he landed on the ledge, but if he missed the ledge there was no way he would survive.

The balls this guy has, thought Al Simon. The cliff face ran about 200 feet from the top to the bottom. At the base of the cliff is a steep slope riddled with massive limestone that fell about 500 metres right into the river. Oscar was right, if they made it down there quick the cops will never catch them..... they were mountain dwelling criminals. This was their element. There was no time to contemplate the risk.

Al Simon quickly removed the money bag and dumped it down to the same spot which Oscar had previously dumped his stash. The money bag swooshed past Oscar without warning and slammed on the rocky floor.

Oscar shot up and saw Al Simon hanging from the edge of the cliff by his midsection, the sole of his boots dangling, searching for a ledge. When he found it, he lowering himself down, while his other foot searched for another ledge.

Satisfied that Al Simon was well on his way Oscar proceeded down, picking his way carefully over the cliff face, maintaining his balance at all times.

While Oscar was observing where he was going and how he was going to get there, Al Simon on the other hand was in a hurry to get there without observing where he was going. Al Simon's competitive edge led him into a predicament; he was moving east over the cliff face when he should have been going south. Twenty feet down the cliff, the toe of his boot resting on a ledge no wider than a one kina coin, two fingers curled around a nubbin of rock, Al Simon was suddenly afraid that he would fall.

"Oscar!" He shouted. "Little help here!" Oscar looked up, "Oh shit Sai! You are going the wrong way!"

"I realised that! What do I do now?"

"Alright," Oscar said. "What you want to do is move a little to your right, and then jump right off the cliff!"

"What? Now is not the time Oscar!" Al Simon cried gravely.

Oscar chuckled. "Sorry, I can't help it. Alright, lower your right foot all the way down as much as possible if you can.

There is a good size hole right there if you can reach it. Good luck!"

"Oscar!" Oscar was no longer paying attention. He continued picking his way down. Al Simon pressed his body against the cliff face and bent his left knee while lowing his right knee as far down as he could. He suddenly felt the shallow depressions and pressed his toe into it. Sighing with relief, he stood up on his right leg, then paused, uncertain of his next move.

The cliff had proven to be deceptive. From the clifftop looking down, what appeared as large handholds were smooth surface up close. The places where he could get a secured hold were spread further and further apart. Al Simon searched all around for the next hold, when he looked down, he could see a good size ledge.

He bent his left knee again and lowered his right knee further than he had ever imagined he could and set his foot down to hold his weight. He then looked around and saw another ledge and a vertical crack at least 15 feet down big enough to accommodate his body. Perfect!

With new found hope, Al Simon crossed over to the crack, crouching inside he let himself slide down, down, down until he felt the crack narrowed. He looked down and saw that Oscar had already reached the bottom and was quickly heading towards the money bag. Picking both of them up and dumping them again all the way to the base of the cliff.

Oscar wasn't waiting. Al Simon realised he needed to make haste. He quickly used the narrow crack and lowered himself further down. At least ten feet before Al Simon reached the wide ledge, an Eagle swooped in without warning and clawed Al Simon's head ferociously; the talons bore into his skull and ripped open the flesh.....almost lifting him off the edge.

He felt as if his skull had been opened up by a lightning bolt. The instant pain was surreal. Al Simon roared with agonising fury as his boiling blood rolled down his forehead.

Oscar immediately looked up, "Sai what is it?."

"I'm gonna murder that bird!" Al Simon cried. "I swear to God!" Al Simon rubbed the blood off his forehead before it reached his eyes. Deep in pain he heard the innocent cheeping of chicks, startled he quickly turned to his left and saw an eyrie in a cliff face tree, with two eaglet, not yet fledgling moving around in there, restless, probably sensing danger.

Apparently, he had come too close to the Eagle's nest. The mother was only defending her nest.

Oscar kept looking up not sure what was happening until he saw the giant Eagle gliding around plotting a second assault, "Sai!" Oscar shouted. "It's coming back! Get down from there fast!"

The pain was unbearable, accompanying it was the blood trickling down, impairing his vision. Without thinking about it Al Simon hurled himself down. Before the Eagle swooped in again, Al Simon was soaring through the air before landing in a heap on his two feet. He was fine. But he wasn't happy. Al Simon stared up at the Eagle motionless, you stupid bird.

Oscar was about to do the second climb down. "Sai let it go! We have to keep moving!" Oscar said, "Come on!"

Al Simon didn't move or hear anything. He kept his gaze fixed on the Eagle that had attacked him. "You wanna mess with me?" Al Simon shot his bloody hand back, grabbed his AK47 and flipped it around. "Nobody messes with me and gets away with it."

He handled the gun with the confidence of someone who had trained with weapons, wasting no time cocking the weapon, and taking a dead aim at the Eagle.

"Wait!" Oscar yelled, but he was too late. The gun roared with rapid discharge. The eagle fell like a dry kapiak leaf..... spiralling down the mountain.

Oscar shot up with rage, "Are you insane!" Oscar screamed, furious. "Now the cops know where we are you idiot!"

Al Simon didn't mind; he was satisfied he shot that eagle. He looked over to the eyrie and saw two innocent heads poking out of the giant nest. Desolated. They will surely die from starvation he thought as he swung his gun back and retreated in one motion.

Chapter 46

At the eastern side of the clifftop, the six Kerowagi Mobile Squad in hot pursuit stopped dead in their tracks at the sound of gunshots coming from the south side of the cliff.

They looked at each other and realised that they were heading in the wrong direction the whole time, "Shit!"

Further up on the roadside, the policemen huddled up and crouched, with their weapons in hand aiming towards the V8.

The officers trained their weapons on the two motionless suspects, one in the far back and the other in the driver's seat. The back doors were open; they looked inside and saw that there was no one else. The money was gone too. The bullet riddled corpses were pulled out from the vehicle and tossed like dogs near the roadside dump.

When the bodies were tossed carelessly, both corpses landed on their backsides, and the hands somehow come into contact with each other, as if someone had thoughtfully placed them on their backs hand in hand.

Even in death, the Rento brothers remained together.

All around people stood speechless at the brutal spectacle before them. The feeling in the atmosphere was one of deep sorrow. The women folks couldn't help it and sobbed quietly.

"The other two are heading east," said an astute officer. "They won't get far. The blood hounds are on to them." By blood hounds he meant the Kerewagi Mobile Squad.

The gang had unfortunately run into the Kerewagi Mobile Squad. The Mobile Squad were returning back from a drug bust somewhere in Dom. The renowned Kerewagi Mobile Squad could hit or miss…..the officer wasn't smiling.

Further up the road, Maria was attended by some policemen and locals. She had sustained a significant head injury. She was fine but badly hurt, and too traumatised to talk. Her body shook all over as she sat motionless while a young doctor who lived around the area examined her as they waited for an ambulance to arrive.

The six Kerewagi Mobile Squad in pursuit of the two bank robbers came to a dead end at the edge of the gorge, and looked at each other with uncertainty. They couldn't see the two fugitives anywhere.

They came to the threshold and looked over, scanning the limestone dominated steep slope…..there was no way the fugitives came this way. But then, "Look! Over there!" Exclaimed one of the officers, pointing south east. "They are crossing the river now!"

The rest of the officers squinted to see the two fugitives well at the base of the gorge traversing the river.

The distance between them had to be more than six hundred feet. They couldn't believe how the fugitives made it down there that fast. One of the officers shook his head in disbelief, he had to ask, "Did they jump down?"

"I don't think so. I think they went down that way." Said another, pointing towards the spot where Oscar and Al Simon had descended.

"Screw this! We have to find another way around. This is suicide. They got lucky, we might not." Said another.

Without warning one of the officers lifted his M16, took a dead aim at one of the runaways below and pulled the trigger. The gun roared three times. The runaway traversing the river fell before the gun roared.

What? The officer stared down over the barrel of his M16, uncertain whether he had shot the suspect or not. He could swear the suspect fell before he pulled the trigger.

Chapter 47

Oscar had almost traversed the river when he slipped on a submerged algae riddled rock and fell awkwardly as the bullets sailed over him. Still struggling at the river, grabbing the rock for support he heard subsequent gunshots.

Accompanying the roar of the next gunshots, Oscar felt a sensation he had never felt in his life..... a bullet sailing past his flesh. There was a hiss of wind, like the backlash of a whip, as the bullets just missed him and exploded in the rock which he was grabbing for support, that exploded with a puff of dust.

He felt his body rise like a sprinter out of a gate. Fuelled only by adrenaline, and barely conscious of his actions, he was suddenly running, hunched, head down, pounding across the river bank to his right. Blood surging, he scrambled, breathless.....turning left and right, giving the shooters a challenge, zig-zagging, trying to dodge the storm of bullets, making his way southward.

His wet jeans felt more restrictive. In the heat of the moment, he had the final glimpse of Al Simon further downstream darting inside the bushes and disappearing. Oscar followed.

When he arrived at the spot where Al Simon had vanished, he kept going, fighting through the bushes, darting inside a cluster of reeds. He was gone.

The shooting stopped as the six officers above contemplated in silence what their next move was going to be. There was no quicker way down, except down over the dangerous cliff face. They didn't sign up for this.

Oscar slowed down, breathless, after realising there was no longer any gunshots. He was wheezing for air as he came to a stop.....he was now looking down at a hollow bushy gap created by pigs. Everywhere at the base of the reeds and bushes was a web of these hollow gaps which pigs used as tunnels to travel around at the base foraging.

There was no other way around the reed barrier; massive clusters of reeds ran all the way up the mountain and barricaded the river bank.

Without hesitation Oscar got on his knees with his AK47 and the money bag in hand and crawled on the putrid path. Oscar could smell the rotten vegetation and pigs' manure on his way in.

Crawling on all fours like a pig. Disconcerted spiders and insects crawled all over his head and face. Oscar crawled about twenty metres into the narrow passage and arrived at an open space.

Oscar quickly rose to his feet with his gun in hand and realised Al Simon could have gone anywhere; Oscar looked around and saw walls of reeds on all sides forming a sort of natural ally or hallway, and there were four different paths which Al Simon could have taken.

There was an eerie silence. The scorching sun was high above his head, the breeze moved gently over the surrounding vegetation.

"Sai!" Oscar shouted. "Sai where are you?!" No response from Al Simon, just the breeze moving through the leaves. Oscar looked around and saw shoe prints on the eastern sandy floor. Oscar immediately traced the shoe print.

He was jogging now, "Sai!" Oscar shouted, wheezing. "Simon! Where the fu -"

The roar of three gunshots silenced him. Oscar ducked to his right. The shots were fired somewhere inside the bushes, and Oscar knew it did not come from Al Simon's firearm. This was a revolver. Al Simon does not have a revolver.

Oscar slowly moved through the labyrinth of reed like a panther towards the sound of the gunshots, silently, darting his weapon from side to side. He knew he was walking into an ambush, the killer would lay in wait, but Oscar had no other option, he was on the run, he had no time to play hide and seek.

After silently moving at least thirty feet to the south he could see the open. He immediately hid behind the bushes. Crouching in the shadows, Oscar peered silently through the bushes, kneeling; he saw the riverside garden some distance from Waghi River, it was the same spot where the gang had shared roasted pig together only hours ago.

The sudden dread in his soul made it hard to stay focused. He needed to keep moving…..he scanned the open thoroughly from left to right until his eyes rested on what appeared to be someone laying out flat on his back beneath the banana trees.

With a sudden burst of energy Oscar broke out into the open. Before he knew it he was running wildly through the riverside garden towards the riverside where the body lay, which was the only exit point he could see; the only way out…..the only escape route.

Striving past he caught a glimpse of Al Simon laying flat on his back. His chest gurgling blood, his body quivered, and he was trying to move. The intensity radiating from Al Simon's eyes in these final seconds of his life was terrifying.

Al Simon, with tremulous effort, lifted his arm, held it out, quivering, beckoning.....before Oscar realised the warning a gun roared once as the bullet smashed into his collar bone .....the gun in his hand dropped right down. Oscar fell backwards, the weight of the drenched money bag dragging him down..... struggling against the pain he rolled over and frantically started back at his gun.

Before he could raise the gun and fire, a foot caught him square beneath the chin.

Chapter 48

Oscar was a man accustomed to pain, this was certainly not the first time he was shot, but the searing heat of the bullet wound in his right collar bone was nothing like what he was used to.

The bullet had smashed his collar bone and missed his carotid artery by millimetres. Writhing in agony on the dirt flat on his back, he opened his eyes, squinting, trying to see, but the sun on his face blurred his vision.

The spear-shaped leaves of reed all around seem to converge in on him.

Out of nowhere a massive dark form stood over him, blotting out the sun completely. When Oscar looked up, he was staring into the barrel of a silver revolver, on the trigger end of the gun Ialasam Gelma stood brandishing his gun, looking almost amused.

Oscar spat on Ialasam's silky dark police boot with pure disgust, "You! I knew I shouldn't have trusted you!" Oscar said, loathing. "I knew you were up to something!"

"Your instincts were correct." Ialasam stared at him, perfectly immobile except for the glint in his ghostly eyes. "You shouldn't have trusted me."

Oscar felt a surge of anger. You killed Al Simon! He tried to move but Ialasam stepped on his chest, pressing him down. Oscar was too weak to move.

"I had all this mapped out. You and your crew fell right into it." Ialasam levelled his gun at Oscar's head. "And now you will die."

Oscar could not breathe. Ialasam tilted his head, peering down the barrel of his gun. Oscar held up his hands in defence. "Wait," he said, slowly. "Tell me why you are doing this? What have we done to you? I need to know that I deserve this."

Ialasam smiled smugly. "That is the same thing they all say, before I put them out of their misery."

The blood drained from Oscar's face. It can't be. It's him! The sudden realisation crashed down on him, Oscar began to feel his world spin. Oscar was now looking at Ialasam dead in the eyes with utter disbelief, "Ghost." Oscar could hear himself say.

"Exactly. You were all fresh escapees on the prowl for anything heavy, gullible so to speak," Ialasam taunted. "All of you. I only needed to lure you in with the score, I knew you above all people could never refuse the action. I want you to know that I have respect for you, but nobody knows I exist.....I intend to keep it that way. Once you are all dead and the money is gone, the cops will arrive here and bare the full brunt of all of this. After all, the public will never believe a rumour about a renegade criminal. I will forever remain a myth."

Oscar could only stare at Ialasam. He was looking square into the eyes of the man who was responsible for killing some of the most Notorious criminals in the Eastern Highlands. What Oscar had thought all along as a fictional character invented by cops to create dissolution in the Highlands Zone criminal underworld was as real as the bullet lodged in his collarbone.

Ialasam aimed his gun again. "There is no regret in killing people who deserve to die, only pleasure.....deep sensational pleasure. Your job here is done."

"Go to hell!" Oscar screamed with rage. "Burn in hell you double headed snake!"

Ialasam took a dead aim on Oscar's temple, "I'm already in hell."

The gun roared, Oscar's brain splattered. Ialasam lowered his revolver and tilted his head as if admiring a work of art. He was relishing the moment. He stood proudly over the corpse and took a long indulgent whiff, absorbed in the all the olfactory function, savouring the scent of death. The thrill of taking a human life consumed him. He seemed at peace with the whole universe.

Crouching in the bushes nearby Dua stared in abject horror at the scene before him.

Ialasam turned slowly and caught Dua directly looking at him, Ialasam held out his hand, beckoning, "Come here Dua," said Ialasam, "Don't run.....Dua!"

Dua ran. He fled for his life.

Chapter 49

Dua was already out of breath when he finally reached the top of the mountain. The desire to simply lay flat on the dirt and catch his breath was overwhelming, but this did not happen. Dua no longer heeded the desire of the flesh; his mind and body ceased to coordinate.

What he witnessed wasn't just murder, it was a pure evil! No one could have been prepared to witness anything like that. The only thing on Dua's mind was to find his grandmother first above anything else in this world. Dua looked back down the mountain to see if Ialasam was following him, but there was no sign of Ialasam Gelma anywhere.

But that didn't mean Ialasam is no longer a threat, Dua had seen what Ialasam Gelma is capable of. Ialasam Gelma was a demon whose path had unfortunately crossed with Dua, and Dua was determined he would make sure he and his grandmother never see that man ever again in their life.

The further they ran away from this Godforsaken place the better.

Dua stood wheezing, contemplating his next move briefly before he went around the hamlet calling in search of Grandma.

Dua was certain Grandma would be sitting outside somewhere waiting for him. Dua quickly paced to the front, and as he had anticipated Dua saw Grandma sitting there on the edge of the cliff, hunching and looking down at the gorge.

Dua called over straightaway as he marched towards her. "Grandma, get up we have to go now, something really bad has just –"

Dua came to an abrupt halt when he realised it wasn't Grandma. It was Susan who turned around to face him. What? What the hell is she doing here?

Susan looked up at Dua without saying anything; her eyes were filled with deep sorrow and pain. Dua could tell that she had been crying.

"What's going on Susan?"

"Dua I – I'm pregnant." Susan burst out. "It's not Thomas's, I can never go back.....Thomas is going to kill me."

"I'm truly sorry to hear this, but right now is really not a good time –"

"Dua I can't believe you are saying this. I thought you loved me!"

Love you? Dua was speechless, whether Susan was crazy or not was certainly up for grabs. If she is pregnant as she claims to be – then the father would have to be the insane murderer he had just run away from because that is the only other person apart from Thomas that Dua knows that has slept with Susan.

"Susan, I don't want any part of this okay, I just want to get out of this place." Dua said. "I just witnessed Ialasam Gelma execute two men in cold blood down by the river –"

"What are you talking about?"

"I'm talking about the guy you made love to passionately down at Wara Simbu two nights ago! Ring any bells?" Dua said, frustrated. "I really need to find my grandmother and get out of this place I don't have time for this."

Susan opened her mouth to speak but no words came out. She withdrew away from Dua, as if she was afraid of Dua more than what Dua was telling her. Dua could sense a strange void. Something in her reaction just didn't add up. She was somewhat genuinely confused and angry. She needed help.

"Look Susan, I understand you must –"

"Dua I never made love with anyone else that night –"

"Susan, I was there I saw it all. I'm not blind, I saw you with Ialasam underneath the bamboo beside the river that night –"

"Dua! I wasn't with anyone else that night! You are scaring me."

Dua needed a moment to process this. Dua was now certain Susan was either crazy or a terrible liar.

"I understand you are under a lot of stress," Dua said, consolingly. "But right now we have to find my grandmother and get out of this place because Ialasam is probably on his way up here –"

Susan sobbed, cutting Dua off. Dua realised Susan was losing it, and for some reason Dua sympathised with Susan. They may not have been lovers but they were good friends, and for that Dua felt obliged to help this defenceless woman who truly is in mortal danger from both directions. God knows what Ialasam Gelma will do to her and her unborn child, not to mention what Thomas has in store. Dua realised Susan really did have nowhere else to go.

"Susan, you can come with me, I will help you." Dua said. "But we have to find my grandmother first, Ialasam could be near already."

"Dua." Susan said, calmly. "That night when I was chased by Thomas and you came stood up for me, we hugged and you left, remember? But you came back to me and we made love beside the river. I don't know who this Ialasam person is…I was with you Dua. I made love to you. And, your grandmother she–

Susan couldn't fight back her tears, she started sobbing, "Your grandmother died a long time ago Dua, she killed herself. You have been living alone here, both Ialasam and your grandmother do not exist……"

Susan's last words echoed. The earth shifted beneath his feet. His whole world spiralled out of control into oblivion. Darkness. Murky. Bottomless well, even the light in his mind blotted out; a world of infinite silence and nothingness.

Chapter 50

Dua stood there in a trance.....time seemed to have lost all meaning on the mountaintop. His mind spiralled backwards in time, to a place long forgotten, an evil place that was chained to rotting memories ..... memories that were hidden from him by himself, memories that were blocked out for his own good up until now emerged like dead frogs from a contaminated pond.

A cry of bitter anguish echoed. Dua could see himself seeing a massive dark bearded man dragging a little boy without an effort like a twig across the dirt.

The boy looked no more than twelve. Malnourished. Powerless. Writhing in agony as he was pulled by his hair.

Dua could feel the boy's pain. The boy's cry was a bitter one from the depths of an innocent heart.

Dua's heart shattered.....he surrendered..... the floodgates of memories burst open inside his head.

The man kept dragging the boy relentlessly without mercy. The hate in his eyes burnt like hell fire. The little boy who was too weak to struggle lay motionless on the dirt as the dark bearded man clamped both his hands with a rope, threw the loose end over the avocado tree branch and jerked the boy up till his feet no longer touched the earth,

"This is what happens when you disobey me!" The man said, coldly. "You are a bastard! I own the very air you breath! I will continue to do this every time you do something wrong until you get everything right or die trying!"

The little boy hung shirtless, his head hung down, his small bones sticking out from his scared and bruised body. He was no longer crying or struggling. He no longer had the will to live. An old woman was wailing bitterly on the dirt.

"Please stop this!" She cried. "He is just a child! You are going to kill him! He is your nephew for the love of God! What kind of man are you?!"

"Stay out of this mother!" The man roared. "This is no nephew of mine! This boy is an abomination, the son of a whore who cheated with a Masalai! This boy should not be treated like a human! Thomas wanted nothing to do with this boy, why did you save this bastard? You should have let his real father take him back!"

The old woman couldn't speak; she fought a lump in her throat which refused to go down. Seeing the cruelty her son was capable of left her speechless. The bearded man went ahead and tied the end of the rope to the tree bark so the little boy stayed afloat, "let him sleep outside like this for tonight," the man said. "If he is not dead by tomorrow then I guess he deserves to live."

"If you hate him so much why don't you just give him to someone else?" The old woman said, painfully. "I can't bear to see you do this to him every day. You are tearing me up inside. My heart cannot take this anymore."

"You shut your mouth or I will hang you beside him!"

"Do it! Kill me! I want to die! I can't take this anymore!" The old woman wailed. "You have created hell here on earth for us. We are better off dead."

The bearded man looked down at the wretched old woman, "You think you will go to heaven when you die?" The man asked. "You think the life after death is better than this?" The old women slowly looked up, her eyes glistening with tears,

"It will be for us. But, not for you."

The man shook his head, "Oh mother." The man said. "Heaven is a myth, Hell is real."

The man walked off without a second glance. The old woman sluggishly rose to her feet and approached the little boy who was hanging motionless. The old woman wailed bitterly. She held his bony feet and kissed them, "I don't have the power to save you Dua." She said. "But I will go up to heaven and ask God himself to save you, if he doesn't, I will walk through the gates of hell and ask the devil myself."

The old woman than walked to the edge of the cliff and tipped herself over. Silence. Infinite silence. Gradually, the bubbles from the bottomless well surfaced, Susan's voice echoed in a far distant place, her call got louder and louder until a dreadful cry awakened him.

"Dua! What have you done!" He, no longer was Dua. He stood there a single man in double view. One and the same.

A flash of lightning followed by thunder shuddered the land, out of nothingness Ialasam stood in front of Susan. His dark eyes roamed the land, till he saw an army of police officers advancing up the mountain.

He moved forward but stopped dead at the sight of Thomas who had just materialised from the bushes beside the path going down the mountain. Thomas was panting and wheezing for air. He could tell Thomas must have run all the way up from Wara Simbu to get here.

Thomas didn't come alone, in his right-hand Thomas held an axe, shoving it forward, blood boiling, "You! Why are you doing this to me!" Thomas cried as he moved closer.

"Haven't you done enough already? Why did you come back here? You have brought nothing but trouble! Now look at what you have done! You are not mine to hell with you –"

Before Thomas could finish his loathing Ialasam reacted with lightning speed drawing out his gun and shooting Thomas in one motion. Thomas fell backwards in the dirt, holding his stomach. Curling. Thomas was still alive, but he was in great pain.

Susan could only watch; she was at a loss beyond measure.

Ialasam walked towards the dying man curled up in the dirt. He looked down almost amused.

Thomas looked up, in his final hour he saw for the first time what no man has ever seen before; he saw both Dua and Ialasam standing side by side, a single man in double view, "What are you?"

Ialasam lifted his right foot and pressed the sole of his boot on Thomas's chest, pressing him down. "Out of suffering have emerged the strongest souls," Said Ialasam. "The most massive characters are seared with scars."

Dua folded his arm and looked completely immobile, "He's going to die anyway, we have to go." Ialasam took a dead aim on Thomas's head, "I want you to enjoy this, Dua. This man is responsible for our mother's death. He tried to kill us when were just infants."

"I know. But I think that's enough killing for one day." Said Dua. "We have to go now. Let him bleed to death. He's already dying."

Susan stood at the back watching. All she saw was Dua talking to himself. It was nothing like what she'd ever seen in her life before. Dua was having a dialog with himself; he appeared to be alone but there was someone else within him. He stood there split in two.

Susan could feel her heart in her windpipe.

Dua turned around and saw a mortified Susan, "What about Susan?"

"Susan is fine, she has nothing to worry about," said Ialasam, "Thomas is gone. She'll be fine."

"What about the baby inside her?"

"What about it?"

"It's your baby Ialasam."

"Correction Dua. It's our baby. We are both responsible."

They could see the advancing policemen were already moving in fast.

Dua walked over to Susan and stood in front of her, "I am sorry Susan." Said Dua. "Hear this, beside Waghi river garden, there is an Erekola with a massive boulder beside it. I marked the boulder with human blood. After some time go to that place and remove the sand and look under the boulder, I left something for you and the child."

Without a second glance or another word they dashed down the mountain.

Susan stood there, pale as a ghost as she watched Dua run down the mountain and disappear into the forest. Probably the last time she would ever see him. She looked over and saw Thomas's lifeless body on the dirt. She was alone.

THE END

NOTE BY THE AUTHOR

Dissociative identity disorder (DID), or previously referred to as Multiple Characters Personality Disorder, is a serious mental condition. People with DID have two or more separate identities. These identities (called "alters") control their behaviour at various times. Each alter has its own personal history, traits, likes and dislikes.

Lynette S. Danylchuk best stated that Dissociative Identity Disorder is the most extreme form of PTSD and is the result of the child's desperate attempt to survive and adapt to an overwhelmingly confusing and cruel world.

ACKNOWLEDGMENTS

A debt of gratitude to my wife Emnarrah for your patience, resiliency, and also putting up with me whilst I was writing this book. To my friends many of whom I've told about this project, and those that have supported me, I am truly in your debt, this book is your work as much as it is mine.

To my good friend and PNG's Finest Film Director Spencer Peter Wangere for your input, and also advising me to submit my manuscript to FNWF2025 for publication.

Most importantly, I'd like to thank FNWF for providing the platform for writers in the greater Pacific such as myself. A sincere debt of gratitude to FNWF Board of Directors, Steven Jones AM, Director, Anna Borzi AM, Chair and Peter Tuckey, Director, and everyone at the FNWF2025 who have contributed to this book.

GLOSSARY

Bilum - Traditional, intricately-woven bags, made by women throughout Papua New Guinea.

Brus – Unbranded home-grown tobacco grown in Papua New Guinea.

Erekola – Casuarina equisetifolia, commonly known as coastal she-oak, horsetail she-oak, ironwood or Australian pine.

Kapiak – Ficus dammaropsis or Dinner Plate Fig. Native to the Highlands Region of Papua New Guinea. The young leaves are eaten as vegetable with pig meat.

Kambe – A term used in the Highlands Region of Papua New Guinea to describe distilled homebrew alcohol.

Kaukau – Sweet Potato

Kunai Garas – Cottonwood grass. Used throughout Papua New Guinea as roofing.

Marita – Pandanus conoideus is a plant in the family of Pandanus. It is traditional delicacy that is highly regarded in the Highlands Region of Papua New Guinea. Widely used in important ceremonies such as feasts and pride price payments.

Pit Mumu – cooking pit or ground oven.

Raskol – Tok Pisin (Pidgin English) word meaning "criminal" or "gang member," derived from the English word "rascal".

BACKGROUND

My full name is Marshall Ericho, I am 35 years old. I have four siblings, I'm the first born. My father (David Ericho) is a Journalist, I believe that is where I got my writing ability. My Mother (Veronica Ericho) has spent a greater part of her life working with NGO's. Both my parents are from the Highlands Region of Papua New Guinea.

I was born in Daru Western Province; right around the fall of the Berlin Wall. My early childhood education was in the Southern Highlands, and later Chimbu Province. I moved to Port Moresby in year 2000.

I did my first year at the University of Papua New Guinea in year 2010. I dropped out of school due to illness. In 2011 I left University and started working. It was during that time that I came across my wife Emnarrah, also my boss's daughter. We are now married with 4 Children, two boys and two girls.

In 2019 I worked as a Research Officer to the former Deputy Prime Minister Papua New Guinea Hon. Davis Steven. I left work in 2021 to pursue my studies at UPNG. In 2023 I graduated from UPNG with BA Degree in Political Science.

I started writing in 2015. I was half way through my manuscript when my computer crashed sometime around 2018, I was devastated, I worked so hard for so long only to have it all just vanished like that. I did not want to write again.

In mid-2022, I collected myself and started writing again. A part of me wanted to re-write the first manuscript that was lost, but another part of me didn't want to go down that road again. I ended up merging ideas from my first manuscript with the second attempt, the result is my final work submitted to FNWF titled 'DUAL'. Otherwise, 'Dual' would have been my second book, perhaps the sequel.

Writing has always been my passion, I've read so many books, I've studied so many writers, and I'm always intrigued by their unique style in writings. I hope to emulate great writers in my own why, put stories that are Papua New Guinean in western context, infuse our traditional stories with a modern tone so not only will people understand, but they must also enjoy reading it. They must feel welcomed. I want to be able to make people feel related, find connection, and appreciate my culture.